SAN AUGUSTINE PUBLIC LIBRARY
Oklahoma crude.
O9-ABI-360

PRINTED IN U.S.A.

OKLAHOMA CRUDE

Also by Marc Norman

BIKE RIDING IN LOS ANGELES

OKLAHOMA CRUDE

MARC NORMAN

E. P. DUTTON & CO., INC. / NEW YORK / 1973

FIRST EDITION

Published simultaneously in Canada
by Clarke, Irwin & Company Limited, Toronto and Vancouver
SBN: 0-525-16995-4
Library of Congress Catalog Card Number: 72-94683

For Bob Wunsch

OKLAHOMA CRUDE

1

I'm aware the public at large holds the plains cowboy to be illiterate and a rowdy, and while the latter is fair enough, the former is not. The cowboys I knew would read everything and anything they could get their hands on, a habit most of them picked up from long frozen winters locked in a line shack where it was either read, whittle, or bugger each other, and of the three, reading was both the most acceptable and the most educating. Whatever words found on paper were devoured, be it the Old Testament or a course in crocheting, and as many shawls came out of the woods with spring thaw as lay preachers.

Among the cowboys, I would say the books most

highly prized and most carefully passed on from hand to hand were the romances of Sir Walter Scott and James F. Cooper, stories of epic struggles and manly heroics. I know they were mine, and I mention all this at the outset to show I have some notion of how a heroic story should go, all the way from its knights and maidens at the beginning to a noble triumph at the end. While I'm not against telling what I know about Lena Doyle and her father and what came to be known as the Siege of Apache Dome, I can assure the reader it was nothing like a romance by Sir Walter Scott, since it was dumb at the beginning and dumb at the end and more or less a mistake all through the middle. This may not be what the reader wants to hear, but it's what I took away from my few months in the oil business, and I stand on it.

To begin with, I'm not even sure of the year, whether 1914 or 1915, though it had to be before the War with Europe, since at the time my adventure began, I was living in a hobo village in Ringling, Oklahoma, and would not have been there had I not been out of work and broke. When the war came, we all got good jobs, so 1915 is a safe guess. Those were hard times, what with money tight and the small cattle outfits being eaten up by the big beef trusts and so sending thousands of working men out onto the road. A lot of them wound up in hobo villages, forty to fifty gloomy men living on the outskirts of a city and cursing the fate that had put them there. The one in Ringling was in a ravine, near the railyard and just high enough to keep the wind out. The city police left it alone, meaning you wouldn't get nabbed for vagrancy if you stayed close, but also meaning no hope of rescue if somebody began to kick your head in, which happened often enough, what with all the hard feelings and bitterness.

I recall it was a cold spring night in the ravine when I first encountered Holder. We were all crouched around our little fires, wrapped in whatevermuch we had. It was late and things were still, except for the sound of a switch engine puffing around the yard and now and then the clank of couplers, when we all heard footsteps and looking up saw an elderly man moving down the ravine toward us, a runty fellow in a black city suit and gray hair thin like a lady's moustache, having some trouble seeing where he was going, and stumbling over the rocks as he came. We watched, saying nothing, which only made him more awkward, and he tripped the last few feet, sliding into our midst on his seat. He picked himself up and dusted his butt with his hat.

"Hello, boys," he said nervously, with what sounded like a British accent. His clothes hung loose on a weary frame. "They told me I could find men looking for employment around here."

For someone nobody had invited, he at least had the right thing in mind. He got passed a tin can of coffee and somebody asked what he was looking for.

"Two or three men who can handle firearms. I can pay seventy-five cents a day, Sundays included."

A hobo with spectacles holding only one lens asked who he was taking on.

"Pan-Oklahoma Oil and Gas."

Well, when you hear a good one, you laugh out loud, and that's what we did, beholding him and knowing what we all knew about that company. In those days, people who gave Pan-Okie a hard enough time would just suddenly disappear, to the grief of their relatives and the mystification of the law, only to be found by a cleaning crew years later at the bottom of some P-O storage tank, long dead but well preserved, thanks to the action of the crude oil.

"You sure you just need two or three?" asked somebody off in the shadows.

"Good old Pan-Okie," sighed this kid cowboy beside me, whose name was Marion. That's all he said, off the top of his head, but hearing him, the old man lit up, figuring he'd found somebody.

"You look like you've done some ranch work," he said. "Maybe Pan-Okie's put you out of a job?"

"Three times, Mister," Marion answered. "Me and Mase here, last three outfits we worked on sold their land to Pan-Okie and shut down a month after we come on. I thought it was us doing it for a while."

"Then maybe you'd like to get some revenge," the old man said hopefully, but I suspect I'm the only one that heard it, since at the same time another voice was roaring out, "And you let the bastards get away with it!"

Changing the subject was George, our Wobbly. Marion turned to him with a hurt look.

"Now what could I do?"

"You could organize, that's what," George roared, about all he ever said. You may recall the Wobblies were trying to make it big at the time—this one had a gearbag full of pamphlets, every one with red covers, with titles like "A Lathe Operator Looks at Capitalism," or "A Lad in the Mine Shafts," all of them dull as sin and the heroes of each always winding up making a speech from the top of some machine. I won't say George didn't have anything in his evangelism, but he himself was so bad-tempered he made an enemy of every man he met, and besides, what his sort wanted was for all of us to unite and be brothers in labor when in fact none of us wanted to think of ourselves as having anything in common with the trash we found ourselves accidentally living with.

"Why should stockmen be any different than the mine workers?" George roared on. "The mine workers know how to organize—they don't get fucked over like that!"

The old man had gotten buried in the shuffle. Figuring to do him a favor as well as the rest of us, I said, "Shut up, Red."

The old man took it wrongly. "Now wait a minute, boys. Red here seems to have a grudge . . ."

We all moaned.

"His name ain't Red. He's a Red. A Red—do you get it?" said a hatchet-faced man.

From the look on his face, it was clear the old man didn't.

"He's a Wobbly," Hatchet Face tried again. "I Won't Work."

With this, George leaped up, fists shaking, ready to take us all on. "The hell!' he shouted. "I'm working plenty. I'm working on the barricades while you bums sit around here scratching your asses."

The man with the spectacles barely missed his head with a rock. George started swinging roundhouse lefts and rights–we ducked and razzed him. Somehow, the old man managed to get in the middle and calm George down.

"Now just hear me out, boys," he pleaded. "I'm aware how you feel about Pan-Oklahoma. And I'm saying I can offer you a chance to get back at them. You'd all like that, wouldn't you?"

That much was true. With a last trade of curses, the commotion cooled–George drifted back to his fire with an air of victory. The old man waited until we were all still and back in our places.

"Have any of you heard of a lady named Lena Doyle?"

Nobody had.

"Well, she's about to start drilling a wildcat oil well on a piece of land called Apache Dome. Pan-Okie wants her land, and they've been pressing her to sell out or sublease, but she's refused, and you know what that will lead to."

A miner looked up. "You want us to kill her?"

"No, no." The old man was horrified. "To protect her. To help her make her stand. She's all alone up there, and I'm looking for two or three good men to hire on as guards . . ."

At that point, he lost us again. He had had us for a little while, but he'd lost us with those two or three good men, and everybody started razzing once more.

"Hell, I'd blow up a derrick or two . . ."

"You don't expect us to fight the Pinks . . .?"

"Pan-Okie don't use the Pinks. Some outfit named Hellman."

"She's got an oil well. Blimey, let her go pay for professionals," George said, mocking his accent.

"You men don't understand," the old guy shouted over the din. "You don't understand—there ain't no money! There ain't even a well yet! She's got nothing but a fourthhand rig on a wildcat tract with no water, and she's putting it up by herself, with her own hands. It's pure speculation—it's speculation. The wages for the men she needs are coming out of my pocket, not hers."

Well, with that, there was only one question worth asking, and we all paused, glancing at each other to see who would get the honor. It turned out to be Hatchet Face—speaking slowly and clearly, he smiled at the old guy and asked, "Then maybe you'll tell us, Mister, since it's so hopeless and poor boy and you're going in the hole for it, just how come you give so much of a shit about this Miss Doyle?"

"Yeah—how come?" said Marion.

But instead of looking found out, the old man drew himself up with a proud look on his face. He seemed very pleased to answer that.

"Because I am Cleon Holder. I'm her father. And she is my daughter."

There are natural limits in the world, and it's a wise man who lives within them. Cleon Holder had just stepped outside his. We had listened to his story at all the way other people go to the opera, as a way to kill an evening, but he was now at the point of overstaying his welcome, and we told him so.

He was angry we wouldn't believe him. "Well, she is! I swear it," he insisted.

"Go home," said Spectacles, reaching for another rock.

"Now see here," he shouted, "I came down here with my cards on the table . . ."

An old, old bum with a mangy white beard threw a cup of coffee fair across his chest.

With that, Holder exploded, suit-tails and hair flying. "I tried to treat you men decent. You're crazy. You know that—you're all crazy."

Every man fell suddenly silent. And with reason—I can't imagine anything worse to say at such a time, especially when you're some weary fart who has just insulted a crowd of unhappy men for not having the desire to commit suicide at Pan-Okie's convenience. I could tell Holder realized this as soon as the words left his mouth, for he turned away, avoiding all those murderous looks, and mumbled, "Well, all right then. I guess I better go try somewhere else, since I can't find nothing here." And he began to leave.

At that, he might have gotten away untouched—after

all, none of us had any love for Pan-Okie and each would have taken not some small pleasure from seeing it burned, but despite his bold exit, we could tell by the shuffle in his step and the way his feet trod on top of each other that Holder was scared shitless. And that's all a bum needs to pounce.

They let him pass among them a little ways until Hatchet Face stuck out a boot, stopping him.

"You got a little something, Mister?" he asked.

Holder was glancing all around, looking for a way out. "You men aren't interested, all right," he croaked. "Let me look somewhere else."

"You must have a spare quarter, maybe," somebody said, invisible in the shadows except for the gleam and click of a blade being pulled.

"This ain't fair," he gasped. "I come here on business."

"I see a watch chain." The source of this deep voice was a huge fellow we all feared, since he was built like a locomotive and about as strong. "I see a watch chain," he repeated, and he loomed out of the darkness like a locomotive coming out of a tunnel, if you can imagine a locomotive with its hand out.

Holder turned pale. "Now you leave me alone."

"No," the huge man replied, and with the shove of one finger forced Holder into a corner of the ravine, with his back against dirt and no friends among the men on either side.

At this point, I stood up, said "Okay," and began to gather up my gear. Everyone turned to me—I suppose

I was as surprised to find myself doing this as any other man, and as for why I was, I wasn't sure, since all Holder had been talking about had made little sense to me. I had at that point maybe one corner of an idea that only got put together long after, but nevertheless there I was, standing and strolling through the fires over to Holder, motioning him to follow me out of the ravine.

Marion was shocked. "Hey, Mase?"

"Huh?" I said.

"Are you with me, or what?" Holder asked, as confused as anyone else.

Instead of going into it there, I pulled at his sleeve and started off, forgetting completely the huge man who sidestepped into my way and grabbed my shoulder like a wolf trap closing.

He looked me full in the face. "I still want his watch," he said.

We glared at each other for some time. Finally, I turned to Holder. "He wants your watch."

Holder hesitated, so I did the only smart thing—I ripped the watch out of his vest and handed it over. The huge man examined it—it was a fair-sized watch, but it tended to get lost in the cracks of his palm. And while he was distracted, I moved out smartly, hauling Holder after, and if someone who was there was to say his feet didn't touch ground for the first hundred yards, I wouldn't be at all surprised because I know I didn't let him go until we were well in the middle of the freight yard and the hobo village was well out of sight behind.

In the light of the carbide arcs that lit the yard, I could see his hair was all on end, like a dandelion in seed. It took him a while to get his voice back.

"That was a close one."

I nodded—no denying that. "She got anybody else working for her?"

"Some Indian, is all," he answered, looking down at his vest sadly. When I'd ripped his watch out, the fob had torn a buttonhole away.

"I guess I should thank you," he added.

Well, I behaved as if he should, but in my mind I knew he shouldn't have. In fact, I was hoping in a few weeks he'd be cursing my name. As I said earlier, I still wasn't sure exactly what I was doing, but I was putting a few things together, one being that I was forty or so and, as they say, not getting any younger, and weak in the chest and lungs from too many Texas winters out in the fucking open, and although I'd never accomplished much of what I'd aimed to do in life, most likely from a want of having any good ideas, the one thing I now wanted to do more than anything else was go down to Mexico, where I knew the sun would dry me out inside and a gringo could live like a lord on pennies a day. And here I suspected, two paces before me, was my ticket, leading me through the dark town toward a little shack he had behind a commercial hotel, going on and on about his daughter Lena up on that dome, surrounded by evil. Those weren't his words—I say surrounded by evil because I recall while he went on, into my mind came one of those pictures from the detective magazines, the kind you used to find in barbershops and such, specifically one titled "Goodness in Peril," which had this young settler lady in her cap and white apron standing beside her slain husband in her log cabin as a ferocious Commanche with a knife in his teeth climbs in the window. I remember this lady because of her unusual posture, which was eyes and mouth wide open in terror, her arms up making a U, and her body twisting and leaning away from the menace in a way no human being I'd ever seen could lean without falling over entirely. That's how the mind works—when Holder talked of his daughter, I thought of this leaning lady.

And I remember thinking, if I stay cool and not get overly clever with myself, there's a very easy and modest con to pull right here.

When I say a modest con, I'm speaking of maybe one hundred to a hundred and fifty dollars, not much today and not all that much then. In fact, the only place in the world it could put a bulge in your pocket was Mexico, which was, of course, my point. And to show how easy I expected this con to be, I earned a nice percentage of it my first day on the payroll.

Cleon was remarkably green for a man of his age and maybe overly impressed by the way I'd handled things at the hobo village, but he still knew full well even if I was Wyatt Earp with a hard-on, one of me alone wasn't enough for his needs, so talking it over, we decided to pass another day in town, in the hopes of recruiting more hands. His idea was to wander among the saloons and beer halls and spread the word he was looking. I told him that was a splendid plan, and while he was off taking care of that, I'd take charge of outfitting myself with a rifle and handgun. For which I would need some cash. And on top of my wages.

That took him by surprise. "I figured you came with weapons," he said.

I only gave him a smile and a shrug.

Somewhat put out, he pulled off his boot after a bit and took a roll of cash from its tip. "You should have said something last night."

"Like what? I'll get you out of this alive, but it's going to cost you an extra fifty?"

"Is that what it takes?"

"For something decent." I was guessing he had no idea himself.

He sighed as he counted the bills out, put his boot back on, then took his hat and left. I gave him a few minutes' head start and walked downtown myself, turning into the first gunsmith I found and telling the man at the counter I wanted the oldest rifle and handgun he had. There was no mistaking me as a collector of historic things from the Old West—muttering to himself, the man rummaged around in the back of the store for a while, eventually coming out with a crate of what first looked like old garden tools but turned out to be weapons, all covered with gunk and rust, their stocks in splinters and all the bluing worn off. I priced them all, putting together the most rock-bottom cheap combination I could find, being an ancient Colt Navy revolver and a long Sharps rifle that looked like something you row with. The two cost me fifteen bucks, along with fifty rounds for each—the gunsmith said at that price he couldn't insure the action of either, but that suited me fine and I walked out of that shop a happy man, with a profit of thirty-five dollars on my hip.

In those days, having pulled off such a neat trick, a man would head for the nearest bar to buy himself a congratulatory shot, and things leading to things, wind up blowing it all, ending up with nothing but puke on his shirt and one more dissatisfied employer to bring him grief in later days of need. But I was showing a strength of purpose new to me. I wanted Mexico bad and instead of boozing, I walked into the Petroleum Trust Bank and opened a savings account, putting it all in. So out of the day's effort, I came away not with a buzz but a 1915 calendar with a picture of a moose on a rock, little to show perhaps, but a good omen for the future.

By the time I got back to the shack, Cleon was there and he looked as satisfied with his day's work as I did. He said he'd talked it up real good in the saloons and had right away sensed a lot of interest among the men. In fact, he said, so interested had the town been that he'd found on going into some beer hall they knew all about him and what he wanted already, the word having spread that fast, although he gave this fact a different significance than I did. Anyway, he assured me all we had to do was relax and choose from the candidates as they rolled in.

The afternoon was warm so we closed the wooden shutters on the shack windows and settled back to wait. Actually Cleon waited, dealing himself solitaire at the table—I went to sleep, which, as I knew, proved the better use of time, since not one single soul showed up. The afternoon dragged on for him like one of those drinking songs with five hundred verses, but then toward sunset, he heard some conversation out in the courtyard and he shook me awake, saying he'd heard someone mention his name.

I sat up and listened. He was right—someone was looking for him, and having a hard time of it from all the knocking and asking he was doing. I glanced over at Cleon and saw him grooming himself, licking his fingers and smoothing his hair down into place, and I suppose I did something like that myself, seeing as I wasn't going to have the sole franchise on this man any longer and I had to make a strong first impression on my competition. So I moved to a chair, leaned back folding my arms, and Cleon picked up a newspaper and shook it open, both of us like we didn't have a care in the world when the knock finally came on the door.

"Come in," Cleon called out.

There was a pause—whoever it was was having trouble with the door latch, but finally it opened and the man stood outlined in the door frame.

Aw shit, I thought to myself—it's Marion.

That's exactly who it was, with some dangling handgun in a tooled belt pulling his pants down off his hips, standing there with a yearling grin on his face.

"Afternoon, gentlemen," he said. "I've been thinking about your proposition . . ."

"What the hell are you doing here, Marion?" I snapped.

His boldness turned to hurt. "I'm signing on, that's what. What's wrong with that? I figured . . ."

I made a face at him that meant shut up or feel pain, and turned to Cleon. "Uh, would you mind stepping outside for a moment," I said.

"Hey, c'mon Mase," Marion yelped.

I gave Cleon a knowing look. "He's a friend of mine."

Cleon eyed us both, chewed his cheek, and then finally nodded. "All right, I suppose–if you think so," he said, and took himself unhappily outside.

As soon as the door shut, Marion began to protest, but I was there first, jabbing a finger in his chest. "I want to know what you're doing here."

Marion drew his boot tip through the dust on the floor. "Well, I figured if you thought it was all right . . ."

I shook my head no.

Marion sighed and wandered off across the room. He spotted my roll and seeing the rifle stock and revolver handle sticking from it pulled them both free, examining them with a sour expression.

"It ain't a good job," I added.

"Then why are you taking it?"

"Because times are going to get worse before they get better."

"Well, I say it too."

He had me there. Everybody had been saying those same words for so many years, my father to me, his father to him, everybody's father to everybody, that they didn't mean anything anymore, surely not as a reason to convince someone of something. I knew then I was going to have to do something with Marion that I rarely liked to do with any man, and that was, level with him.

I took his arm and sat him down. "Now listen up, Marion, and I'll spell it out. Here's this woman all alone in the middle of nowhere with this oil well."

"Aw, you don't believe any of that . . ."

"Now just hush and listen. It don't make any difference what the truth is, Marion—whether she's really rich or poor, or whether she's alone or has forty boyfriends up there with her—it still is someone weak going up against Pan-Oklahoma. Correct?"

He nodded, waiting for my point.

"All right, then. I figure there has to be money to be got out there, either from the lady and the old man for carrying guns for them or, just as good, from Pan-Oklahoma for laying them down . . ."

Marion's face brightened when he saw the beauty of the setup, and was about to say so when I cut him off.

". . . but first of all, God knows what a man will have to go through to get any piece of it, and . . ."—and I stuck this in quickly because I could see he was about to say something like, I'll go through the fires of hell to grab a few bucks if it's with you, Mase old saddle-pal—"and besides I don't want to split it with anybody."

That stopped him short. He glanced up at me from under his eyelids in a way that made me groan.

"Is that your last word?"

"Aw shit, Marion."

"I thought we was pals, Mase."

"Something will turn up for you."

He nodded sullenly and drummed his fingers on the table for a while. "Okay then, if that's the way you want it, Mase. I ain't going to argue with a friend," he said, still trying to twist the knife. I only got up and opened the door for him.

When we stepped outside, Cleon was there, humming and doing things that showed he'd been trying to eavesdrop at the door. His face fell when he saw Marion stick out his hand to me.

"Anyway, shake hands, Mase. No hard feelings."

I shook back firm, making sure to grind his knuckles a little. "Sure, Marion—see you around."

Marion hesitated but then walked off without a further word. I mumbled something like, "He wouldn't have worked out," to Cleon and went back into the shack.

Cleon followed me inside, downhearted. "Wouldn't have worked out," he repeated.

I shook my head.

"He was my last hope."

"No—actually, I'd say I am."

Cleon nodded to himself, knowing that was indeed so.

I am not the sort that discovers pretty bugs and flowers in a mud puddle, so I can't be expected to have much nice to say about an oil field. I realize there are those who can, but I suspect the nearest they've ever come to getting the miserable stuff out of the ground is to watch the man in the bow tie pour a quart of it into the crankcase of their automobile. I suspect those who can see beauty in a landscape are usually those who've never been involved in grabbing something from it, for I have seen Oklahoma from the oil business and from the cattle business as well, and I can tell you if you take away all the derricks and put back the tall green grass and fill the land with heads of beef, I see only so many cows' assholes needing to be kicked in one direction or another for a hot fourteen-hour working day. I think you can say that in general about people—there's a former lumberjack here who feels the same way about a pine-covered hillside, and there's a former Seattle fisherman who once told me he'd never seen anything more disgusting and depressing than the Pacific Ocean.

Now the field around Ringling was about as ugly and typical as any when Cleon and I drove through it on a one-horse buckboard the next morning on our way out to the dome. It was your usual boom field—derricks platform to platform, each with its own walking beam creaking up and down and its own steam engine puffing like a little volcano, and everything coated with oil—men, machines, what trees were left standing. What the picture books don't reveal is how badly it stank, not only from the oil but from the crud in the slushpits and the lakes of salt water spreading over the ground and pooling under the platforms, and any open space that didn't have oil or crud or salt water had a pile of rotting garbage started by some crew, who were never known for their hygiene. That was the famous Ringling-Hayworth field, but you don't have to check my facts because every one was like that, from Burma to Coalinga.

At any rate, I wasn't paying much attention to the scenery that morning, considering as I was how best to meet and manage the young woman. I hadn't much practice dealing with a boss lady, there not being many in those days. Women were soft and sacred things to us, and we put them up on a pedestal, though I suspect that was only to get them out of sight of the terrible things we did to each other at their feet. In fact the only lady I'd ever worked for had been when I'd signed on with an outfit run by a big fat guy named Mike Mitchell who could arm wrestle any of us down and who ran the show like Julius Caesar, except that around the thirteenth of every month, he would disappear into the hills for a couple of days, and it was a while before I found out Mike was really Mary and she'd go off in the scrub with her monthlies. From what Cleon had told me about his daughter, she was the other kind, the "Goodness in Peril" type, and as we bounced along, I was giving a lot of thought to how best to gain her confidence, the way you might tame a forest doe, with smiles and sugar.

While I mused, we passed through the field and out the other side into the landscape. You could spy an occasional rig here and there out to the horizon, mostly dusters, test holes bored outside the field by independents who couldn't afford to lease space inside. The land was useless for farming or ranching, the topsoil all blown off, gullies cutting up the land in every direction so it looked like an apple left out in the sun. Cleon had been trying to make small talk for a while but now he shut up, I supposed because we were getting near the place. Everywhere you looked, the land was fenced off with barbed wire, and on each fence was a little stenciled sign reading, "No Trespassing–Property of Pan-Oklahoma Oil and Gas."

We drove through a clump of low hills and when we came out into the open again, there was the dome maybe a mile ahead. It was your classic anticline dome, a hundred feet high, all on its own, almost perfectly round and smooth all over, rising like a tit out of the prairie except that it was baked brown and covered with a stubble of dry weeds, with a Pan-Okie fence running in a circle around it. On the very top I could make out a tar-paper shack and near it an oil derrick lying on its side on the ground, a short one, substandard, maybe forty feet in length. As we came closer, I saw it was positioned on one side of a platform already constructed—to the other side of the platform was a gin pole sticking up in the air, with all sorts of gun-tackle blocks and pulleys on cables between the pole and the derrick top, and going the other way, another tangle of blocks and cables between the pole and what looked like some sort of hoisting engine on the ground. It seemed we were just in time to help with the raising, but at that point Cleon reined up in the cover of a little stand of trees bordering the road and sat there, just watching.

This struck me peculiar. "Don't you want to give her a hand?" I asked.

He mumbled something like, it's better to wait a while, and appeared uneasy, which, when I thought back, had been his state for the last hour or so. But he was boss and it was all the same to me, so we just rested in the shade.

Being closer now, I could see the hoisting engine wasn't the usual steam engine or steam tractor but some cockeyed hit-or-miss gas engine bolted to the bed of a Ford flat-bed truck. It couldn't have been over fifty horsepower—they didn't make them any bigger then—and though I wasn't any engineer, I'd done enough hoisting and hauling to know that lash-up couldn't raise a midget in his socks, but apparently I was in the minority because as we looked on, we saw the woman mount the bed of the truck and crank the engine over and somebody else, obviously the Indian Cleon had mentioned, stand over by the derrick and make gestures with his hands. When the engine was chugging as good as it could, the Indian gave a sign to lift and the woman put the engine in gear. The cables went slowly to taut, meaning at least they had a winch with some reduction on the engine, and then took up the strain.

Well, when you're lifting from horizontal, the first ten degrees or so are the hardest, not only because gravity is working totally against you but because you have the worst angle on the thing to be raised, even with a gin pole to take some of that angle away, and usually there's a few odd seconds when everybody holds their breath to see whether the thing goes up or comes down on their heads. Those on the hill stood still, looking on, and I suppose we on the wagon were just as still. A few seconds passed—there was a terrible creak we could hear all the way down to us, and I suddenly saw daylight between the truck's wheels and the ground. That's what was happening—something was going up in the air all right, but it was the truck, not the derrick, winding itself up on its own cable. The Indian waved his hands like crazy and the woman threw out the clutch

—with the strain gone, the cable sagged and the truck fell back with a crash, practically staving in two and raising a big puff of dust. I chuckled out loud at the spectacle and turned to Cleon, but he was long-faced and silent. Picking up the reins, he gave them a slow shake, and we rode up to the fence.

Being now at the base of the dome, we didn't have a line of sight on the top, but I figured we must have been seen as we came, having raised dust of our own. I started to get down to open the gate in the wire when Cleon stopped me.

"It's best to let her know who we are first," he said.

That still sounded strange to me, but I figured things were always strange when you were new on a job. And after a moment or two, there she appeared, outlined on the ridge. I couldn't make out much of her except that she seemed young and slight, with wine-bottle shoulders.

"That's her," said Cleon, and he stood, waving his hat. "Hey, Lena," he shouted. "It's me—Cleon!"

At that point, something distracted me—I remember looking down at the left-hand trace and noticing those two inches of leather had parted, all of a sudden, even though we were at rest. And then I heard a little pop in the distance and it will be to my eternal shame that it took me all of five seconds to put the pop and the trace together, to realize that a bullet had parted it, that "Goodness in Peril" had a large-caliber rifle up on that dome and she well knew how to use it better than most marksmen I'd run into.

We both stayed there for a while, me with my mouth

open, Cleon frozen in the middle of his wave like somebody in a snapshot clowning for the camera, with two or three odd slugs zipping past or taking chunks out of the buckboard seat before I hauled him down by his collar, stuffed him under the seat, jerked as hard as I could on the right-hand lead and hollered at that horse, practically leaning forward to his ear. Well, the beast threw his head and started digging with four legs all at once, and we spun in our own tracks, executing what in the military we called a 180-degree counterwheel, meaning every man for himself, and back down the road we flew, the three of us—me, Cleon, and the horse—each practically counting out loud the paces between us and the stand of trees we'd left behind.

Once back in cover, we all stood panting, catching our breath. The horse was angry at both of us for the ill treatment—I myself was only interested in Cleon, in how many different ways I could make him pay, how many ways I could fold him in on himself the way you take a piece of paper and see how small you can fold it. He had suckered me completely and I was well outraged at having been taken in.

"Your fucking daughter, huh?" I screamed in his face. "Your fucking daughter who's all alone and needs fucking help!"

"She's suspicious . . ." he said, trying to pull away from me, but even he knew how awfully stupid that word sounded.

I held him there by his collar, truly about to kill him, the nerve of him having conned me into such a thing. But something stayed my blow—I recalled I had conned him yesterday, and furthermore planned to tomorrow, which made me pause, took some of my steam away, and I suppose saved his life. I lifted him and banged him down on his spine, disgusted at the sight of him, but otherwise let him go.

When he saw I wasn't going to do anything more serious, he drew himself up and smoothed down his clothes. "I haven't been completely honest with you," he said.

All that warranted from me was a dirty look.

"I suppose it's fair I tell you all the facts," he went on, and began to relate to me what had happened two days before.

The truth was until two days before, in fact the day of the night we'd found each other, he hadn't seen his daughter at any closer than a fifty-yard range for twenty-five years. The truth was, he'd run out on her mom and her when she was two years old, when they were living in Detroit, Michigan, an action that had pleased him at the time but brought him guilt and remorse ever since, and in a guilty, hang-dog sort of fashion, he'd kept track of his daughter as she grew, watching her ups and downs over the years, which were many, since her ma had died of TB when she was ten and she'd been thrown out in the world on her own. Cleon had gone his way, which he admitted had never amounted to anything, and she'd gone hers, into the oil business, or at least the way a woman can be in the oil business, which is mainly limited to being kept by oil men, but he'd managed from time to time to have his path cross hers, always with the idea of presenting himself and making his apology and peace with her, but he said something had always stopped him whenever he'd gotten close—either she'd be doing better, in which case he'd be afraid to spoil things by putting in an appearance, or else she'd be in bad shape, at which point he wouldn't want to add an extra burden to those she was already carrying. He'd known her recent years had been downhill mostly and he knew, feeling up against it, she'd put all she had left into this dome, leasing it for pennies long before anybody else was seriously hunting oil in this corner of the state, and while she'd sat on the property over the years, he'd sat on her in a sense, waiting in the background, hoping she'd reach a point where so much help would be needed to bring in the well that he'd finally have an excuse for reintroducing himself. And what with Pan-Okie after her land, he figured his time had come.

It wasn't amusing to me at the time, but Cleon must have hung around some of the same barbershops I had, because even having seen her on and off over the years, he had the same "Goodness in Peril" notion of her I did, thinking of his daughter in the way he remembered her best, namely a little pink lump in a blanket, and was greeted in the same way as we'd been as he walked up the dome road that morning, namely a well-aimed slug covering his trousers with dirt. She naturally enough didn't know him from Pope Larry and was shooting at anybody who came through the fence.

He said he yelled her name and his name over and over, but she was well dug-in behind a little mound, and even as he shouted his own words, he said he could hear the click of another round being chambered. So he called out, "It's me, Lena—Cleon Holder. I'm your pa!"

She threw another slug at him out of reflex before she paused. He spread back his coat to show her he wasn't armed.

At that point, she slowly stood from behind cover, looking this way and that like a bird on a branch, sure it was all some kind of trap. But seeing nobody, she moved down the slope, keeping the muzzle well on him, stopped, and looked him square in the face. He must have seemed familiar, because she made a sigh and sat slowly down in the dirt, putting her face in her hands.

"Oh Christ—what are you doing here?" she whispered.

It wasn't the greeting Cleon wanted but it was something, and it gave him heart. He scuttled up toward her, keeping shy of that big Winchester musket. He said it was all he could do not to reach out and touch her.

"I know how you must feel," he said to her.

She just snorted, so he went on, explaining how he knew about the jam she was in, how he knew in fact a lot about her because he'd looked in on her now and then.

This peaked her interest, but in the wrong direction —she asked him for an example, and when he mentioned some time in East Texas a few years back, she blushed red all over and was bringing up the musket again when he added quickly he'd only seen her and the gentleman at a distance and had passed on, since she seemed to be doing well enough on her own.

As he was talking, Cleon said his eyes drifted down to her hand gripping the musket stock. He said he went soft all of a sudden, something like swooning—the hand was just like his, short and stubby, which didn't mean anything to me, but he assured me it's the kind of thing that moves fathers, seeing themselves in their kids. So he stuck out his own hand toward hers and said, "Look at your hand, Lena. It's just like mine."

Once again she misread his intentions and swung hard with the butt, smashing his fingers. In desperation and close to tears, Cleon shouted, "Look at it, Lena—we got the same hand! Lena, goddamnit—I come to help you!"

"Me and my oil land, you mean," she yelled back.

"No—nothing like that. To help you—to help you hold out, if that's what you want."

He said she chuckled. "Help me do what? Can you handle a rifle?"

Cleon couldn't—a lot less could in those days than is today believed, so he only shrugged.

"Handle a derrick, maybe? Make a hole?"

"I can learn . . ."

"Just get out of here," she sighed, cutting him off cold.

He couldn't move. He'd come there with just one idea in mind, an idea he'd nursed for years, a great idea to set everything straight, and here was his daughter, at last before him, telling him the idea was no good. He couldn't move—he just stood there like a stump and said, "No—I won't."

She yelled in his face. "What the hell good are you?"

"I'm your *pa*, Lena!" he yelled back.

"So? You going to read me *nursery rhymes?*" she roared, and with that, got up and headed back up the slope, leaving him there.

Cleon said he practically died in that moment, that if we are all corruption, he had never felt more like something rotting than at that moment. Lena wasn't kidding—she was going to do it without anyone, including her natural father. He shouted after her, "Lena! You can't do it this way."

She stopped and looked back over her shoulder. Speaking very clearly, she told him to fuck off.

Now it's my contention that of all the weapons in a lady's arsenal, her strongest is foul language. Not a man's—in the case of men, the saying sticks and stones can break my bones applies, because only the coward fights with his mouth, while the brave man speaks with his fists. In the case of women, it's exactly the opposite—I know lots of fellows, especially scrawny ones, who just love to drive women to blows, knowing the runtiest man can usually take the strongest woman in a fistfight, seeing as a woman lacks something in coordination and always throws her punches like she throws dough onto marble, overhand, early seen and easily blocked, instead of the man's way, the straight jab flicked from the shoulder. On the other hand, you watch a frilly little thing tell some bruiser to take a flying fuck at the moon and she'll stop him in his tracks, with a look of shock all over his face, his edge lost, and probably mumbling something silly like, "You ought to watch your language, you know." I don't know why this is—it's merely a fact of life I'm noting.

At any rate, I could well imagine what Cleon felt when his own daughter addressed him that way. All he could reply was, "Please don't do this."

"I mean it—fuck off!" she repeated.

He said he fell down into the dirt, on his knees, almost praying. "I can't, Lena," he moaned.

Her face turned red and she thumbed back the hammer on the musket. "GET OUT OF HERE, YOU SCUMBAG SON OF A BITCH," she screamed, and from the hip threw a shot that sent him flat.

He said he knelt there with his eyes shut, waiting for the bullet in the brain, almost welcoming it, because without his daughter and having failed at everything else in his life, there really was no good argument for his hanging around any longer. And glancing up at her from beneath his hat brim, he could see she was just about willing to provide it. Just about.

But she didn't, so after a long while, Cleon simply got to his feet, brushed the dust off his sleeves, and started down the hill. But it was all wrong, he realized as he walked, he was going away and alive when where he really wanted to be was here with her, even dead, but as he turned to say something to that effect, she emptied the musket's magazine into the air—bang, bang, bang, bang—as fast as that, the noise drowning out whatever he was saying, so he walked off without a further word, not looking back again.

Well, after he finished his tale, we were both quiet for a while, him I suppose because of the pain of going over those events once more, me because I was working hard to change my notions to fit the new facts. The second installment of those hundred and fifty was going to be a lot harder to harvest than the first, it was clear, Lena being what she obviously was. I was going to have to think this out a little. And while we sat there, each with our own thoughts, a faint sound came to us—the lifting engine cranking up again.

We looked at each other, got down from the buggy, and crept around the trees. It was true—they were going to try it again. As far as I could see, the only change in the arrangement they'd made was to load a dozen or so full gas drums up onto the bed of the truck with the idea of anchoring it better. To my mind, they were still in trouble, since the change gave them no more lifting strength, but sure enough, they took their positions again, the Indian gave the same hand signal, and the cable went taut once more. As the winch clanked and the engine puffed, I kept my eyes on the truck wheels, waiting for them to rise. They did, slightly, but to my astonishment, with a long creak of wood twisting, so did the derrick on the other end of the hoist. The Indian was whooping and jumping up and down for joy—the derrick was actually lifting, reluctantly, inches at first, and then, as I've pointed out, with the angle becoming more and more favorable, foot after foot, through ten, twenty, thirty degrees of arc and going faster.

I could see the next problem arising already—once you get something that large and heavy moving, you've got to give some thought to stopping it far in advance, by slowing down the rate of haul, and most likely by having laid some guylines to hold it erect, or else the thing in its perversity will travel all the way through the vertical and come down in your lap on the other side. But Lena, who was working the winch, only picked up on this fact of engineering late in the game, when the derrick had climbed maybe sixty degrees. She eased on the brake, knowing enough not to slam it on and thus snap the cable, but it was too late—even with the winch stopped, the thing kept whistling up on its own, with the cable falling slack and all the blocks banging together uselessly, and passed through vertical, heading down the slope on the other side. With a yell, Lena jumped off the truck bed fleeing for her life—the Indian did the same, but just then the derrick's legs caught on the sort of chocks crews would build into the platform for that same purpose, creaked loudly, and the whole tower tottered back in the direction from which it had come. There the other two legs ran into chocks on the other side, and after rocking back and forth unsure for a while, the derrick settled with a satisfying thump into holes in the platform that had been prepared for it.

We could hear two distant voices cheering. There it was, just forty foot of wooden tower, but standing all alone atop that barren dome, looking awfully tall with no other upright in the neighborhood to compare it to. It was an achievement too, no matter how many ways you could pick apart the particulars. Lena had done it, done something next to impossible, and as she'd vowed, done it next to alone. And I recall this well, as we sat there looking at that derrick pointing up to the sky, we each tied it in very closely to Lena's reception of us, since in silhouette that derrick was making a gesture to us known from coast to coast.

Cleon glanced over at me, and I suppose he saw the concern in my face, because he said, "Now listen, Mason—you still got your job . . ."

"You're fucking well told I do," I snapped back, wondering where he'd got the idea that I didn't.

4

Now I suppose if I have to name my profession, it's working with riding mounts. I didn't know this at the time, but looking back on my life, it occurs to me I spent more time with horses and donkeys than anything else, which is nothing to write home about, as anyone who has been around them can witness. Still, I learned a few tricks in those years and I used one to reach the top of that dome alive.

It was what you did with mustangs, in catching those wild ponies of the plains. The story has it they could smell a hunter before they could see him, but in my experience they were always too busy rutting and eating to smell anything, the crucial thing being to move in on them unseen. We'd do this by waiting until early morning or late afternoon and closing with the sun directly at our backs, and I decided to use the same device with Lena Doyle.

I couldn't see killing half a day with Cleon there in the trees, so even with sunset far off, I hopped from the wagon with my weapons and headed away, telling him to stay there until I called him. There was a little wash paralleling the dome road–I crawled down it on my belly for a spell until it swerved off to the north and figuring I had to move around to the west eventually, went where it did, and it obligingly took me around the base of the dome to the far side. Spitting dust and sneezing, I lay studying the slope. It looked favorable–a nice smooth approach, a soft curve, with the occasional knoll or dip for cover.

The secret was to have the sun directly at your back. Try it sometime, standing on high ground a half-hour before sunset and turning full circle–you think you're seeing everything, but notice how your eyes hurry past the sun and a few degrees either side of it. That's human nature, and that's what I was counting on, those few degrees, giving an extra little percentage to the fact that the Indian and not the lady would be lookout, and knowing what failings his race was prone to. So I put myself in what looked like a line between the sun and the dome top and raised the rifle vertical on that line before me. It threw a shadow, but off the line, off to the left. That meant I was truly not in line after all, so I crawled maybe thirty feet further down the wash to my right and did the same thing. This time the barrel's shadow was to the right so I split the distance back by fifteen feet and when I tried it, the shadow pointed directly at the tar-paper shack like a finger.

I sat there in the dusty wash for a few hours, working up a sweat and playing games to pass the time, such as having races between the drops from either armpit and betting on which would reach my waist first. It was a long dull afternoon but evening finally came, and with the sun about a hand over the horizon, it was time for me to move out. Nosing through the weeds, pulling the rifle after, I slithered under the barbed-wire fence and up onto the slope itself, pausing behind a little mound. There was a dip between this mound and a third of the way to the top—figuring the chance was worth it, I hauled up and sprinted the distance, puffing and chugging up the incline, throwing myself down into a nest of nettles when it began to flatten. The nettles stung—cursing them, looking and listening, I picked my next stop, a tuft of grass maybe twenty yards ahead, and crawled safely to it.

Closer to the ridge now, I could see its details—the rim nearest to the tar-paper shack hung out over the slope a little and it occurred to me if a body could get below that overhang, he could hide neatly as long as he wanted. So I started for it, but at that point saw the Indian coming around the top walking kind of mournfully with a rifle cradled in his arms, not looking like anything I couldn't handle, but then an alarm was as bad as a repulse, so I squeezed flat and gave him a good five minutes to pass, which he did, his feet moving and his body not, as if he was on rails. Taking another chance, I covered that last distance in a loping crouch and chucked myself well beneath the overhang. It was another hour or so until the darkness was on us–if that Indian had had a mind to, he could have walked out onto that overhang and looked down and would have seen me smiling stupidly up at him, all curled up like some big dusty baby, but I was gambling on the fact he wouldn't, and he didn't.

Lena spent the last minutes of daylight commencing to rig the derrick, and when night fell, she crossed into the tar-paper shack, locking the latch behind her. She must have made herself some supper because I could see smoke coming from the stovepipe on the roof. The Indian stayed on sentinel, making his rounds in an unhappy way, knowing it was an almost moonless night and to the advantage of my kind more than his. I waited a while more, until the lantern went out in Lena's shack, and then crept out of my hidey-hole, laying in wait for the Indian below the rim. He rolled around a few minutes later–I let him pass, clambered up the last few feet to the top, stepped up behind him, and laid the sharps on his shoulder right near his neck. He froze–I reached past him, carefully took his rifle away, and turned him around, putting my finger to my lips.

He wasn't scared. He knew I had him cold, but if anything, he looked annoyed, as if he'd been waiting for me a long time and I'd just wasted his by taking so long. I surprised him when I only shook my head and said, "Run along now."

He didn't get it at first. I said it again, in a friendly enough way. Finally he nodded and, without a word further of thanks or otherwise, hopped over the rim and dropped out of sight, racing down that slope like a man set free by the pirates.

Of course I wouldn't let him know it, but I was almost as relieved as he was, neither of us sure how much of a threat the other was. With him gone, that left only Lena. I crossed to the shack and listened by the door. Nothing could be heard, so with my rifle I pried the door open and slipped inside.

She wasn't much of a homemaker, from what little I could make out in the darkness. There was junk piled everywhere: tin cans on the floor and cooking grease coating the timbers. There was a strewn table in the center with a lantern on it and a box of matches close at hand—shuffling to the middle of the room on the flats of my boots, I picked up a match and lit it.

It took a while for my eyes to focus, and it took even longer to locate Lena. She was wrapped up in blankets near the stove, but there was so much other stuff lying around she just blended in and even when I stepped to her, I could only see the top of her head, the rest of her body looking like a dead fish done up in newspaper. I smiled and opened the window over her, stuck my head out into the night and hollered "*Holder!*" at the top of my lungs.

She jumped up, or would have, had she not been so

well swaddled. For an instant, she stared up at me–I could hear the motors starting behind her eyes and when they kicked over, she flung off the blankets and lunged for something. It was an old horse pistol on a crate–I kicked it across the room, gave her a wink, and called her father again.

She just crouched there, with a look of hate and violence almost outside my experience. I sat on the edge of the table.

"Hi," I said, rubbing it in her face a bit. "Your pa hired me. I'm the new protective agency."

She was in no mood for humor, so I motioned her to move outside. She wouldn't budge, still sitting there glaring like a beacon, so I rolled my muscles a little and made gestures with the rifle. She finally stood and walked through the door.

A few yards from the shack, I told her to sit, having made sure there was nothing near for her to sit on. She looked first at the cold ground, then at me, but realizing her helplessness, finally obeyed. We could hear the jingle of harness on Cleon's buckboard as it climbed the hill, so we both waited silently for him to arrive.

He wasn't that happy with what he saw as he reined up and tied off the horse. I could tell he was uncomfortable, the way he said hello to her in a shaky voice and when that didn't draw any response, added, "How are you, Lena?" She only glanced up at him and sneered.

"You . . . appear well," he said, still trying to get something going, but she turned away, looked me straight in the eye and asked, "How the hell did you get up here?"

"I walked up the road," I answered. "I was carrying a pink umbrella and I had a dog on a leash."

She started to rage, but Cleon stepped quickly between us. "Aw, Lena . . ." he began, and then turned to me.

"Can't she get up?"

I liked her on the ground, but I only shrugged. Cleon tried to help her rise—she shoved his arms away and stood on her own.

By his voice, Cleon was getting desperate. "Lena, it's going to be hard . . ."

"It's been hard already."

"I know it has. So maybe you need somebody more on your side."

She had a way of looking you over like you were something swimming in brine in a gallon jar, and that's the look she gave me.

"This?"

"Aw, Lena." Cleon was close to tears. "You got to trust somebody."

Well, that was the key that opened her up. "Oh sure, Daddy," she said, setting her hands on her hips. "I get yanked out of the womb with a pair of pliers. You take off two years later, and then when I'm ten, my mother dies, and some goddamn reverend's telling me it's because God has more need of her than I do. You bet I've grown up a trusting soul, my daddy."

Cleon looked like he'd been kicked in the nuts. It

was time to step in—I cleared my throat and said, "It seems to me . . ."

She let me get that far and told me to shut up. I only nodded, smiled, took a breath, and began all over again.

"It seems to me . . ."

This time she groaned with disgust and walked off to the side, so I continued, following after. "It seems to me the only thing worth talking about is the fact you and the Indian didn't blow me to shreds on my way up."

That was my best punch—I threw it first, and it seemed to have effect, because all she did was mutter, "Maybe next time."

"You can see how it kind of spoils your argument," I added. "I mean, about carrying this all off alone."

"He's right," Cleon stuck in, waving his hands at me to press on.

"I brought my own gear, lady. I can live off on my own—you don't have to have a thing to do with me."

"He'll give you and the Indian more time on the rig," Cleon added.

"That's right. He hired me, and if he turns me over to you, it's you I take orders from. It's logical—if I'm taking his money, I'm obliged to do the job he wants."

"An honest wage for an honest day's work," she said. "That's what you mean."

Cleon and I both nodded, and looking back, I suppose I must have nodded a little too cleverly, because she smiled at him and then at me, and in a pleasant voice, answered, "You two are so full of shit . . ."

Well, lady or no, I wasn't going to take that, and strode toward her to tell her so, but Cleon grabbed my arm and shushed me. She'd turned away again and was pacing back and forth.

"Let her get used to the idea," he whispered.

She did appear to be thinking the proposition over. Cleon held his breath—when she turned back to us, it seemed she'd mellowed a bit.

"He does any job I give him?"

Cleon nodded yes, yes, up and down.

"Including general housework . . ."

"Spell that out," I said.

"Dishes, laundry . . ."

"Hey . . ." I said.

"I've hired guards," she shouted. "I've hired big, strong men. What I've never had is a big, strong, housekeeper, and that's what I need right now. Do you want the job or not?"

Well, just as I had had her before, she had me now. Of course I wanted the job, painfully so, what with my scheme and Mexico dark over the horizon, and there was no gain in hiding it. So I finally shrugged, letting the dishes and the laundry slide.

Cleon beamed, practically two-stepping there in the dirt. "Then it's all settled. I'm pleased, Lena—I really am."

"Good."

"I just wanted to help you."

"I know that."

"And maybe he can guard a little too?"

"If it don't interfere with his other work."

"That's fair." He turned to me. "Right, Mason?"

"It's fair," I grunted.

"Fine." He turned back to her. "Where would you like us to camp?"

She beamed back. "Oh no. If he stays, you go."

"But . . . but . . ." was all Cleon could say.

"Nothing's changed," she roared. "You said you wanted to help me! Fine–you brought me him. Now . . ."

Cleon raised his hands in a gesture of surrender, knowing even after this short reunion what would happen if he tried to force an issue with her. "All right, Lena. I know. I won't ask no more," he said, and climbed slowly back up on his buckboard as I went around in back to unload my gear.

He sat there looking at Lena with this terribly hurt face for the longest time. Then he forced a smile and said, "Well, I'm very happy I could help you in any way."

He couldn't stand to hear her reply, so he just nodded curtly at me, picked up the reins, and drove off, around the dome top and down the road into the dark again.

Have you ever seen the way prizefighters eye each other across the ring before a fight, as they snort and sniff and stretch their arms on the ropes? Her there and me here, that's how we looked at each other at that moment.

But the bell for the first round didn't ring, at least not for the first few days, for aside from some curt words and some fingers pointed this way and that, she had nothing to do with me, her mind being entirely given to the preparing of the derrick, which for me was all so much mumbo jumbo. She gave the impression of knowing what she was up to, although looking back, it's clear she was mostly faking it as so many of us do throughout our lives. True, she was going through the motions of drilling for oil, but with equipment so old and so worn out as to make success hopeless, her need to do the whole thing herself having put her into a box, because she could only do it herself with old, sleazy equipment since she didn't have the money, and lightweight to boot since she didn't have the brawn, while all around her, the only people who were hitting the pools were those with equipment that was new, expensive, and heavy-duty. She knew something about oil production, true, but from the outside, from having watched from the carriage or listened in the bedroom, which meant she was more sucker than sharpster from the outset, the man who sold her the ancient rig having included in the package, for example, two bull wheels and no band wheel, a fact she didn't pick up on and one she had guaranteed nobody would be around to point out. But this all came to light later—in those first few days, I truly believed I'd signed on with a legitimate oil company, and made my plans accordingly.

It was a challenge for me, this new game of playing both ends toward the middle. On one hand I was honestly employed, on a salary, and if nothing happened, I would someday in the future collect my wages and thank father and daughter for an easy few months. But I couldn't bank on that—any day the daughter might give up, as anybody in their right mind would have done long before, and there I'd be on the road again, with not enough for Mexico surely, and not enough to impress anyone on this side of the border, which meant I was also depending on Pan-Oklahoma to show up in decent time and give me my chance to turn traitor.

It seemed sure they'd come from what I could get

out of the Indian, who strolled up the hill one morning, picked up a saw, and began to build a shelter for the Ford without one word spoken. Up to three or four weeks earlier, the Ringling representative of Pan-Okie had been showing up regularly at the first of the month with the same sublease, all up and up, giving Lena a nice cash advance and the usual eighth royalty. Naturally she'd chased him off, and this month's visit had been missed, which I took as a sign of stronger medicine arriving soon enough.

As for Cleon, I learned the first day he was out of sight but not out of mind. That morning I was poking around in her garbage dump, a little gully running off the ridge, coming up with a gunny sack of tin cans. Then what I did was break off some sticks in three-foot lengths, walk about halfway down the slope, and make a little picket for us all, the sticks spaced around the circumference of the dome, string tied between them at about a foot's height, and the tin cans hung in pairs on the string. It might prove some use at that, I was thinking, if somebody clumsy came up the slope unseen and dragged his feet across the string and set the cans to jangling.

While I was busy with that, and whistling as I remember, since things, despite some hitches, were going my way, a reflection caught my eye. I shifted to the side but the glare followed me, and looking off I could see it was coming from the trees Cleon and I had hid behind the previous day. And focusing my eyes, there he was, holding the hand mirror that attracted me and waving a greeting with his hat—run off but not away, apparently camping out down there to see how things fared with us, but far removed, like somebody up in a far balcony. I waved back though with less enthusiasm—I could understand why he was sticking around, but I didn't like any more audience than I had to have, and I wondered how he might figure in at the fateful hour.

For three days Lena and I grunted and nodded at each other like a couple of hogs as we each went about our business. Of the two of us, I admit she was the less bothered by that state of affairs, for though there were a number of times I might have wanted to start a conversation, the way people in the same pickle do, she showed no similar interest, and had I not learned to yield ground to her as we met, she would have surely walked over me rather than around. Now normally I would not have given a shit one way or the other were it a man, but the truth is, I was thrown off by her behavior at first, because as I've said, the only lady boss I'd worked for had been old Mike Murphy and with her, if you didn't like something she was doing, you could ask her to step behind the shed and take your chances. But Lena wasn't that tough, bullish sort of woman, even though she cropped her hair and slept in her boots. That she had once been a lady showed through all the sass and grease—she wasn't that bad looking, being in her mid-twenties and middle height, though how the curves went beneath the mattress-ticking of her overalls only God, of all of us on that dome, knew. Still, she gave the sense of doing all this struggling and fighting under someone else's lead, as though there was a man inside her telling her what to do but leaving it to the girl on the outside to figure out how. I think I suspected some of this at the time but then I was of no mind to let her know I did, and so soon resolved to give as good as I got and keep up the cold shoulder as long as she would, which can be shown by what happened a few evenings later.

I was doing the dishes—yes, I was sticking to my end of the agreement, out in the open, out by a stack of thin-walled casing pipe they called hen's skin, dipping the plates and cups in a soapy pot and wiping them clean. She and the Indian were pulling the hen's skin up into the derrick with a drawline, the Indian on the winch, her tying the rope hitches and guiding the lengths to their resting place against the inside of the tower. It was dirty work, the casing being used and oily, and I suppose I was getting some small pleasure in watching her grapple with the stuff, getting gunk all over her face and arms and the slick rope continually slipping out of her hands. She knew where I was sitting and how I was grinning, but she ignored me, clenched her teeth and kept on with the job.

At one point, just to make chat, I cleared my throat and said, "You know, you could use another line of barbed wire around the top here."

"That's your department," she answered curtly.

At that moment, the hitch she was tying came loose and the rope flicked across her face, leaving a black line and a nice red welt that must have hurt behind it. With that, she spun around, raging at me.

"You see, the difference between you and me is that I've been dirty and then I've been clean—I mean real clean, with dresses and jewelry and furs—and then I've been dirty again. But you've been just as dirty your whole damn life."

There was nothing I could say to that, being totally true—I continued to grin. Pissed at me and everything else, she flung the line around the length again, cinched the knot, and waved to the Indian to haul away. But she'd done another bad job, because when the casing lifted a few inches, the knot unraveled and the casing dropped back on the stack with a clang, except for the squishy noise it made when it hit her fingers resting on the next length down.

Well, she turned green, she screamed, trapped there—and she looked over at me desperate for help. I glanced up, grinned once more, and went back to my dishes. This may sound cruel, but after all she'd set the rules, not me, and if she was going to get my help, I was determined she was going to ask for it.

That lady stood there in pain, green changing to blue, eyes boring into me, and never said a word. It was the Indian running over who finally set her free and, holding the bent hand, led her off to the shack to see to her wound.

Nothing was said of the incident at supper that evening, although the hand was wrapped up in a rag, and I went to bed contented, feeling my point had been made. Nothing was said in the next few days, which were uneventful, me alternating watches with the Indian, five hours on and two off, with a longer spread during the night. We watched and waited and walked that ridge, but outside of an occasional wisp of smoke from Cleon's campfire, nothing was seen, while behind us two, up at dawn and long into the night, Lena climbed the tower and set her rigging, game hand and all.

Now it may seem strange for a man who's lived an active life like myself to say this, but I have given more thought and work to the state of my bowels than anything else, and moments of seclusion on a hopper here and on a pot there throughout the Southwest are among my happiest memories. I can't tell the reason why, except to say that in Indiana where I was born, nobody talked about anything but rain and shit, so it may have something to do with my upbringing. I make this point because it's what I am—there's something about crapping, something to do with the body running along all by itself leaving the mind to relax and drift, but without the gumminess of sleep, that I have always enjoyed, and having said that, will belabor the point no further.

The facilities on the dome were less than regal, being a classic Chic Sales trestled out over the ridge rim so the droppings could slide down the hill, and for all I know, onto Pan-Okie property, and it was precisely there, with me squatting that afternoon in an off hour, pants around my ankles, face in my hands, that Lena chose to take her revenge.

Out of nowhere, the door flung open, the light flooded in on me, and there she was, her eyes casting up and down. By reflex I reached for my pants tops, but as I pulled, she planted her booted foot right in the crotch and forced them to the floor again.

When is a man more open? She knew this and let me stew, which I did for a moment, before I got control of myself once more.

"Hi," I said, friendly enough. "Need something?"

She didn't blink an eye. "About the other day . . ."

"Oh yeah. How's your hand?"

She didn't answer—instead, she exposed her good hand, which had been hidden behind her back, and in it was her horse pistol, and she leveled it right at my head.

You know full well my grin faded. "Hey, lady . . ." I said, my mouth suddenly dry.

"What's wrong?" she smiled.

I couldn't begin to answer that. "Don't . . . fool around."

With that, she brought the muzzle to my nose. I watched rigid as it traversed my face and disappeared out of sight around my right side, but I could feel its coolness by my ear. And holding it steady there, she fired.

I don't know how others react to loud noises, but I remember that explosion, that bang alone, was like a mule kick in the mouth. I must have leapt up and tried to flee that echoing privy, but while the top half of my body was willing, my lower half was trapped in my own britches, and all I did was crash face first outside onto the ground, shouting in pain and pounding away at my ear with my fist. Through a haze, I could see the legs of her overalls marching smartly away, leaving me to suffer unaided.

Now I tell that story surely not to boost myself but to prove to anyone who still thinks of Lena as a lady he himself could bring into line, wild but surely tamable by the man who knew how, exactly how full of horseshit he is. At that moment, I changed my attitude toward Lena from one of indifference to one that could rightly be called fear, and I'm not ashamed to say it, since it seems most natural and to be expected.

From then on, I decided to keep my mouth shut and do my job, knowing I was totally outclassed by this woman and not likely to get any better. It was its own kind of hell, walking around that dome top, eating, sleeping, day after day, knowing she was watching me pass and using me the way I've seen cowboys tear a funny drawing out of a newspaper and tack it over their bunk, as something to give them a laugh in an odd moment. I found another shift taking place in my thinking, and that was, between the two sides, Lena and Pan-Okie, I was definitely beginning to lean toward a run-in with the second, for no matter how many guns they came with, they'd be in the hands of men, a species I could still convince myself I knew something about.

But Fate was staying up late figuring out new pleasures for me, and even though I'd conceded the fight already, Lena and I still had a final round to come.

After a week of scorching days, Oklahoma, as it will, decided to lay on a summer storm, and it waited until one night when I was on watch all the way up the derrick to do it. Imagine somebody cutting a slit in the bottom of a bag of shot and you'll have an idea of what those raindrops were like, and add a chill wind and you have my idea of the outdoor life. I huddled up as best I could under my poncho, watching the rain sluicing off the brim of my hat like water down a gutterpipe, cursing it and the need for me there, for outside of the moments when lightning flashed, you couldn't see your hand, much less an enemy. I knew I was the only person above ground for fifty miles—certainly, the animals were under cover, and looking through the darkness down at Cleon's stand of trees, I couldn't see any sign of a fire.

By the time I was well soaked, I heard a noise and saw the Indian climbing up on the crown pulley to relieve me, wordless as usual, so I nodded and worked down the ladder to the ground. I'd rigged up a little tent for myself near the shack out of a tarpaulin and a pole I'd found, and it was there I slogged, the rain having in a few minutes turned all that loose dirt with no green growth to hold it together into a rich gumbo mud. I reached the shelter, threw off the poncho, shook the water off of me like a dog, and lit a candle.

Now those Good Cowboys I hear on the radio in

the evening always take precautions against this sort of thing when camping out on the broad prairie, but I suppose I must be counted among the Poor Cowboys, for I had taken no precautions, and that tarp leaked like a net and all my possessions—bedding, clothes, and gear—were floating in five inches of water. Even the bank calendar, which I'd hung on the center post, had fallen to the floor and turned to pulp. I stomped about furious in the puddles—on one of my revolutions, my sight happened to pass through the gap in the tarp and land on her shack with its windows yellow with light and its stovepipe smoking merrily, meaning that if the crew was suffering, at least the boss was dry. But there was nothing for that, so I stripped down and cursing stretched out on the ground, pulling those soppy blankets up around my chin. Oh, I was doomed that night—that was clear—so I forced my eyes shut, tried to ignore the water dripping in my face, and commanded my body to sleep.

Well, I commanded for maybe fifteen minutes and at the end, jumped out of bed, yanked on some clothes, gathered up gear and bedding, a few cans of food, jammed my hat on my head, and stormed through the rain toward her shack, with no idea what I'd do when I got there but all sorts of reasons driving me on. I lost some nerve when I neared the window and beheld her there in person, cooking at her stove, but at least in this encounter, forewarned was forearmed, so determined this time to either shout her down or knock her down depending on the need, and taking a deep breath, I banged the door open and barged inside.

And she turned, her eyes narrowed and her mouth opened, but I didn't give her a chance.

"Now it's pouring outside and my tent leaks—all my gear is wet and all I want to do is dry off so I don't catch the grippe and wait here for the Indian."

Coming on fast like that worked. She couldn't say a thing.

"Look at me, Lady," I pressed on. "Do you think I want to do anything more than dry off?"

I could see her running over possibilities in her mind, but surprisingly enough, she chose not to say anything and simply turned back to her cooking. I moved to the stove myself and carefully hung up the bedding and gear to catch the heat, all the time waiting for her to start in, on my toes ready for the repulse. But she only hummed a little.

"What I want to do now is cook this soup," I said, "so you tell me when you're done with the stove, and I'll move over where you're standing and you can eat someplace over here. All right?"

"You overestimate yourself," she answered, in a chummy tone.

"I'm just trying to stay out of your way."

But seeing as, for some reason, she was unconcerned, I moved to the stove, opened the can lid, and poured the stuff into a pot I'd brought along for the purpose. And since she was humming, I hummed a little myself as I set the pot down and stirred the contents with my finger.

There wasn't much maneuvering room by the stove, and from time to time in the course of our business, we'd almost touch. As usual, she was the instigator—she moved around the place as though I was transparent. Whenever our eyes would meet, she'd just smile sweetly.

Her beans were warm so she took her pot to the wood table and started in. My stuff was ready soon after, so I announced, "I'm ready to sit."

"Anyplace you like," she cooed.

Now it was of course full obvious she was setting me up, that she had some sort of game going, her same old game with some new rules that were up to me to figure out, but my choices were either to play or leave, and going back in the rain was out of the question, besides which I'd done all right for myself so far and thought that, primed as I was, I might pick up these new rules a lot faster than she thought. So having been given any seat in the house, I sat down directly across from her, our bowls practically touching, and shoveled my soup in in perfect rhythm with her.

After a while she looked up at me, mouth full.

"What's your last name?"

"Mason. Mase," I answered, in the same offhand way.

"Oh. What's your first?"

"I never cared for it."

At that she smiled again. Oh, she was probing all right, but I was ready. In fact, I decided to strike first.

"Where do you come from . . .?" she started to say, but I cut her off.

"I've been meaning to ask you something."

She paused—then nodded to me to go on.

"Is it just the three men I've seen you with? Or do you kind of hate the whole race?"

She kept on chewing her beans, nice as you please, not twitching an eye.

"I never thought much of men."

I wiped my chin with my sleeve. "Maybe you're the kind that prefers the company of women?"

By rights, that should have sent her to the ceiling, but she only shook her head slightly. "Women are worse. Most women want to be men but they don't have the nerve."

"So you don't care for men and you don't like women," I said. It wasn't too clever, but I was stalling. And I was also beginning to sense something was wrong—I was handing out the shit in this contest, but somehow she wasn't being touched. She smiled again and I smiled back, my brain roaring behind that smile, reaching for her gist. But before I could speak, she did.

"I suppose if I had the choice I'd want to be a third sex. In between the other two."

"A third sex."

"Uh-huh."

I didn't like the way this was developing at all.

"This third sex. Which . . ."—and it was hard for me to say—"which sex organ would you choose to have? The one that goes in or the one that goes out?"

"Oh, both," she answered, not even taking the time to consider.

"That's asking a lot."

"Both. One of each."

I was squirming now. "I see. But which would you . . . favor?"

"Oh both. Both equally."

I was in over my head once more, and as usual, with no idea where she was leading me. I looked away, hoping for an end to all this, but having worked so hard setting me up, she wasn't going to miss closing the trap.

"Certainly. If I had two sex organs, I wouldn't need anybody else. I could fuck myself."

The soup that sprayed from my mouth like water from a burst steampipe went all over the table, even onto her overalls a little, but she didn't mind that, eyeing it as a sort of trophy. I tried to wipe up some of the mess. She watched me coldly, her nostrils flaring, that sweet smile all gone.

"Well, couldn't I?"

I balled my fists, and then forced them open again. It was time to leave.

"It's been nice, lady," I said, standing, gathering up my gear and bedding in a big bundle and, as fast I could short of sprinting, heading for the door.

"You're leaving your soup," she said as I passed. Seeing as I didn't answer, she added, "I thought you wanted to dry off?"

"I'm dry," I said, and was gone, out into the rain.

And as I trudged toward the swamp I was to sleep in, I was saying over and over to myself, roll on, Pan-Okie. Roll on, Pan-Okie, and bring me deliverance.

6

My prayers were answered within a few days—I don't remember the exact number but I do know, at least in this one case, my expectations proved correct, because when Pan-Okie finally did come, it came strolling, and it took that dome the way kids catch snails.

They arrived on another rainy night—by mutual consent, the Indian and I had changed our lookout from the derrick to the top of the truck cab, it not making much difference in weather like that. And as hard as I had guarded that night, the first notice I had of their arrival was the Indian shouting from the hole he slept in, which was behind me and which meant they were already among us. To our credit, it turned out they'd driven up and parked their vehicles, a closed touring car and a van, in Cleon's stand of trees only feet from him, but in the rain's clatter had not spotted him nor he them as they moved past. And to my credit, I wouldn't doubt a leg or two struck my picket string on their way up, though the jangling of a couple of tin cans could have never reached my ears in the pelt of that downpour.

There was the bang of a door being kicked in, a scream, and a gun going off. My revolver was handy—the question of course was, and had always been, who to point it at, but the fact we were infiltrated already stacked the deck against a stand for Lena. I needed to know more about my situation so I lit a match under my poncho, brought it to the end of one of a bunch of railroad flares I kept handy at my feet, and flung it over my shoulder.

It hit, washing everything in a red glow, illuminating three or four men in derbies and black slickers, one wrestling with the Indian, the others hauling Lena squirming and yelling out of her shack by her hair. Finding themselves discovered, the four drew their handguns and fired wild into the darkness, and from the darkness came a few more muzzle flashes, which told me there were maybe six of them and that the situation was already decided.

While the bullets whined, I slipped off the wagon and snuck around the rig. To be convincing, I had to put up some kind of struggle—the best seemed at that moment to be along the lines of firing a few shots, wounding somebody, backing myself in a corner someplace, and surrendering honorably, having drawn blood and done my damnedest. In the light of what flare was left, I saw a large, heavyset man standing alone in the middle, obviously in charge the way he barked out orders, dressed in a full-length duster and a cap with goggles, with a mutt yipping at his heels. I decided he'd be the target. He was big enough to hit easy—I'd crease his leg maybe, or his arm, fall back to the derrick and let them surround me. I moved up a few more paces toward him for luck and thumbed back the Colt's hammer. The big man must have sensed me coming, for he'd begun to turn when I fired.

There was an unusual sort of report and the rusty pistol blew up in my hands, knocking me down as it filled my chest with its respective parts. I sat there in the mud, dazed, feeling the blood start to ooze down my front, feeling all those little stabs beginning to flow together into one great pain. The heavy man just shook his head at me with a pitying expression. I was mortified—before I passed out, I remember thinking what an awful mistake this whole adventure had been from the beginning.

When I came to, I was in the back of the van and we were teetering and jouncing down a bad road at a fast clip, every bump sending little nail points through my top half. Lena was there, looking pale and tense, and so was the Indian, with a black eye and some teeth missing. Sitting near the door at the back were two of the Hellmen in derbies, as it turned out, Moody and Dullnig, Moody being very tall with tiny eyes and Dullnig being built like that brick shithouse of story with a face that displayed about as much intelligence. They grinned at me when I came out of it, but said nothing.

I felt my front—the blood was still running freely. I tried to inspect it but my vision was off, so I slid over next to the Indian.

"How does it look?" I said, pointing to my chest.

"I don't know. How I know?" he answered, true to his sullen nature even in danger.

So I moved to the other side near Lena, but she divined my purpose and turned her back on me before I could ask. In the end, I simply tore off my shirt and wiped myself clean, finding a score of gouges but none that deep, the blood having washed most of the metal out. I made a motion to have her see what I'd gotten in her service, but she wouldn't, huddling there in a corner, arms and legs turned in, at this point totally concerned with herself.

The road got worse and we were bounced off the walls for a while, and then we stopped. The boys in derbies herded us out the back—we were well in the middle of nowhere, in a grove of twisted blackjack oak somewhere by a river, still dark and the rain still hammering. We huddled together in the open, away from the dripping trees. Looking behind us we saw the driver of the touring car get out, pop an umbrella, and open the car's back door. With some difficulty, the heavyset man in the duster stepped down holding a briefcase and let the driver, whose name was Bliss, escort him under the umbrella to the van where he mounted the stairs, his dripping dog, who'd gone for a frolic in the mud, following shortly after. He said something to Bliss—Bliss sloshed through the downpour over to Dullnig and repeated the order, and with this we were all prodded back toward the van, the Indian and I to stand near the rear wheels while Lena was taken inside.

For me, this was now a time of delicacy, the issue being over and decided, and I figured it would be useful to overhear what was going on in the van. There fortunately being a crack in its plank sides, I sidled toward it without upsetting the guards any.

Inside, the heavy man was having Lena sit and trying to make her comfortable in a good-natured way, but Lena wasn't responding, as far as I could hear. The van creaked—I figured that was the heavy man taking a seat himself.

"Miss Doyle, I am Captain Walter C. Hellman, U.S. Army, retired," I heard him say. "Currently retained by the Pan-Oklahoma Oil and Gas Company of Philadelphia and Tulsa, and authorized to act for the company in specific matters. This is my letter of introduction." There was a pause, and then he added, "Are you sure?" meaning as I guessed, Lena was ignoring the letter, being in her democratic way as tight-assed with him as anyone else.

"You haven't answered our recent correspondence," Hellman went on.

"Just what do you want?"

There was a sound that told me Hellman was going through his briefcase. I pressed my ear to the opening.

"Okay. Now this is a draft of a sublease contracted between you and Pan-Oklahoma transferring to the company all oil and mineral rights for a period of ten years on tract number 15-R17-T23, for which you receive a cash consideration of five thousand dollars and a one-eighth royalty on all sales of oil and minerals extracted from 15-R17 etcetera, otherwise known as Apache Dome."

There was a long pause. Then he added, "This is a fountain pen, Miss Doyle. You're familiar with its use."

"I got ten-tenths now."

"Ten-tenths of what? An anticline dome in Oklahoma. Now some people think there's oil underneath . . ."

She laughed out loud at that.

Hellman clucked his tongue. "I'd like a nickel for every smug bastard who knew he was sitting on the mother pool, when all he drilled was dusters. Until you find oil, you are speculating."

"If it's so worthless, why do you want it so bad?"

"Pay attention, Miss Doyle," he answered, "I didn't say worthless. Not at all. All I'm saying is, if you drill dust you're wiped out—you've lost your investment. Whereas a major oil firm can afford to drill a thousand holes, and if one decent well comes in, it's covered costs, and if it gets two, it's making a profit. A major company's got a margin for error, and you little independents don't. Now examine this sublease . . ."

The van creaked again—he must have been moving nearer to her.

"You get it both ways—you stick the firm for five grand, which is yours to do with, and you make twelve percent off the firm's profit on the land they lease from you."

Once more he paused—she still wouldn't answer. When he spoke again, a little edge was creeping into his voice.

"You paid four hundred dollars for that lease three years ago . . ."

"You pay five thousand and make five hundred thousand . . ."

"Yes, and our distributors make five million. You surely can't expect all of it, Miss Doyle." He sighed loud enough for me to hear it. "Look, dealing with us don't have to be a headache, you know. There was a poor dirt farmer by the name of Wilson. He held out for a while, but finally signed—we became pals, him and I. I just received a postcard from him the other day. You know where from?"

Lena wouldn't guess.

"St. Petersburg. On his royalties alone, him and his wife are taking a trip around the world. Can you imagine that? St. Petersburg—home of the Czar."

He let that sink in for a second. "What do you say?"

"Give me the pen."

"Ahh," said Hellman. Something rustled, probably the lease. "Right there at the bottom."

A moment passed. I don't know exactly what she wrote on that lease–I'll always regret I never thought to ask her–but it was enough to lower Hellman's voice a couple of octaves and get his teeth showing. His fat friend act hadn't worked with her–I've heard that saying about inside every fat man there's a skinny man wanting to break free, but I would say in the case of Hellman, inside him were five more big fat men, each one meaner than the next, for there was true destruction in his voice when he read what she'd written.

"I hope you don't mean me personally," he said quietly.

That new voice threw her as well as me, because when she answered, her voice wavered. "I didn't mean you," she almost whispered. "I meant everybody." And I heard her start to cry.

"It's not good business to cry. Sign it, Miss Doyle," said Hellman.

She just sobbed.

"That's the thing about women in business. They tell you to treat them like a regular guy, and when you do, they start the waterworks on you."

"I'm not *crying*," she shouted all of a sudden, and from her voice, she wasn't, at least not anymore. "I'm not crying," she said, in a calmer tone. "It's my land."

There was another creak and the van body swayed–the door in the back banged open and Hellman was standing over me, motioning to Bliss to take her away.

I looked past his legs—Lena was sitting there rigid, totally surprised by Hellman's abrupt move. She blanched as Bliss and Walker squeezed past Hellman into the van—now she lost her nerve and screamed as they took her by the arms and legs and dragged her toward the door.

"Don't hurt me," she wailed, as they shoved her past Hellman.

Hellman shook his head. "I don't see what else there is to do," he replied, stepping back in the van and shutting the door behind him.

Lena's terrified face caught mine as they drove her toward a thicket of trees. I looked away—I, of course, could do nothing for her, and was in fact giving all my thought to my own neck. Hellman was as bad a number as I'd seen, and it was looking less and less likely he'd be interested in my proposition, but then, this moment was what I had sought and I had no one to blame but myself, so I went up to Walker and told him I wanted to speak to his boss.

Walker kind of chuckled, but still knocked on the door and passed on my request. After a second, he ushered me in.

Hellman was standing when I entered. He looked bad enough in a landscape, but in the confines of the narrow van, he was surely awesome the way he seemed to fill an entire end, hips, butt, and shoulders. And to frost the cake, his mutt Bull was at his side, growling at me with clear intentions. But Hellman only batted Bull aside with his hand and motioned me to sit, which

I did as casual and matter-of-fact as I knew how, even with water dripping off me and pooling around my boots.

His briefcase was beside him—also a collapsible tin cup which held some coffee. He saw me eyeing it and asked if I wanted any. When I told him no, he shrugged and pulled out a silver flask to freshen his up. The flask was empty—he turned and knocked on the little sliding door between the van and the cab, but there was no answer. He looked somewhat put out—he called for Bliss and we waited for him to come.

Through the drum of rain on the roof, I could hear Lena screaming in agony from a distance, and those screams kept coming, over and over. They unsettled me, those screams, indicating the boys were truly working her over in a professional way, something I hadn't thought they'd bring themselves to doing. I was relieved when the door opened and Bliss was there.

"Where's Bloom? Rucker?" Hellman demanded.

Bliss answered a little awkwardly. "They went over to watch. They've never seen . . . you know, a woman . . ." meaning it was new ground for them as well.

Hellman nodded and waved him away, settling for what was left in his cup. He let me fidget there for a moment or so with nothing but Lena and the rain to be heard.

"You ain't going to kill her?" I asked.

"No," he answered, his only word on the subject. "What did you want to see me about?"

"Business."

He nodded at me to go ahead.

"I've been working for Miss Doyle. But I don't owe her anything . . ."

"That's wise."

"When I heard about her situation, I figured I'd make me some money. I figured either she'd pay me to help hold her property or somebody else would pay me not to. It appears you people are on top."

He smiled, seeming to appreciate the realistic way I looked at things. "Speculating," he said.

I nodded back. That was it exactly.

"How much were you expecting?"

This was tricky, this business of numbers. I thought for a moment and said, "Not much. Say two hundred."

"And then what?"

"I'd go my way."

Well, I thought he was taking me seriously, the way he leaned back to consider. And why not–after all, he was a businessman and I was a businessman, and it was just business we were discussing. So he thought some, and then turned to me, friendly enough.

"Look, let me ask you something. If you had to, could you be satisfied with one hundred?"

Well of course I could, but I wasn't anxious for him to know it, so I took my time before I allowed that I could, if that was all there was.

"Would you take fifty?" he asked.

I was in trouble. I stood to leave, but he seized my coat.

"Would you take ten?"

Now the question was simply getting out of there. While I searched the van for another door or maybe a window, he went on.

"You see, I'm given a budget by the firm. Asking them for extra funds to pay off people like you would show bad faith on my part. My word to the firm means a lot to me."

"I'm just trying to get out of your way, Mister."

"I appreciate that. But it's finished. Pan-Oklahoma takes possession of that dome this very morning."

"It ain't your land."

Hellman just shrugged.

"People might put up a fight," I added, it being the only threat that came to mind.

Hellman nodded in agreement. "Of course–it happens all the time. But not by your kind, though. A man running around saying buy me, buy me, is not anything to worry about."

Well, by then I was pretty scared and my damn hands were making things worse by shaking out of control, but I still knew from some similar occasions in the past there was a pattern to this sort of thing, and the next action called for on my part was a large bluff. So I simply yanked my coat out of his grip and started for the door, all insulted.

"Wait a minute," he called out. "How about this for a compromise?"

A compromise? I stopped. Jesus, anything at this point–fifty bucks, I thought.

"Like what?"

"I give you five bucks and you kiss my ass."

The only thing left on the agenda was for me to kill him, which I commenced to do with scant hope, leaping for his throat. He gave me a shoulder, smartly for such bulk as his, and let go of the hold he'd been keeping on Bull's collar. Bull lunged, sunk his teeth into my arm—I threw him off and fell back, him snapping after and forcing me toward the door. Holding the dog away with one foot, I knocked the door open, only to find the Hellmen in a grinning semicircle below, waiting for me.

Dullnig was closest on my right hand—I caught him in the face with a boot heel, and when he went down, leaped over him and away, falling to the mud and struggling for footing. From behind, Bliss swung a sap —I blocked it and managed to lift a fist to his gut, with little force but well aimed, and it took his breath away. Walker roundhoused, which I ducked under neatly and managed to shove him off balance. When I got up, I was a half-step ahead of the others—making for the trees, feet flying and digging for traction, I gained another.

And then I stopped cold. There on the ground before me was Lena, bloodied, her clothes ripped off, her body twisted and swollen, her face half-sunk in the mud. It was that awful sight that undid me—at that instant, there was a swish and a sap landed behind my ear, and I went down in a heap. My last two memories are Dullnig kicking me over and over in the ribs and

Hellman sticking his hand out of the van door, palm up, to see if it was still raining.

And what of the poor Indian? I was the first to wake the next morning. The rain had stopped and the sun was out. The birds were singing, the river looked lovely, and hanging limp over its ripples was the Indian, the rope around his neck running to a stout oak branch. And then I passed out again.

7

Beaten and out of my mind as I was, I shouldn't be expected to recall any of my first thoughts upon coming to for good, but the fact is, so strange were those thoughts that they've remained with me ever since. I recall them because they were about revenge—they all had to do with getting back at those who had done me, taking care of those bastards in their derbies one by one, each a more lingering death than the next, with me in a dreamy way tracking them down to saloons here in Arizona and card tables there in Louisiana, finally cornering Hellman himself, those tons of him quivering in fear, telling him who I was with a smile, and as I leveled my pistol at him, asking if he recalled a little fracas once at a place called Apache Dome. I wouldn't doubt I smiled there, sprawled where I was on a dusty settee, wrapped in all those good thoughts.

After a while, however, the clouds parted and I found the sensible part of me wondering where all that had come from. Revenge? No, this part said—the best I could hope for was they wouldn't come after me to complete the job they'd begun, and any space I could put between us would be all to the good. Revenge? No chance, never. Take it out on someone else down the line, perhaps.

Then I recall what amounted to a third voice saying, "On the other hand, none of this means anything if this fellow is dead, which hasn't been proven one way or another." Everyone agreed this could be done by my opening my eyes and drawing some conclusions, but as simple as it seemed, my eyes had notions of their own, preferring to stay in a sort of heavy nowhere rather than use the energy to find out anything final, and it took me a long time to coax them open.

I saw my settee was in the parlor of a small frame farmhouse, filled with bric-a-brac and plow parts, and there were three people near at hand speaking at a table. Two of them I didn't recognize but one looked somewhat familiar, and I finally decided it had to be Cleon, strangely enough. And growing more conscious, the pain came back—looking down, I saw I was stripped to my skivvies and my legs and arms and chest and shoulders were all wrapped with strips of torn sheeting, so I looked for all the world like something about to be shipped somewhere.

I must have let out a groan because the people at the table stopped talking and turned around. The man I didn't know passed me over a bottle of Peruna. I gulped some down and then sat myself up.

The man, who seemed to be a farmer, what with his muddy boots, was going back to his conversation. "It don't surprise me none," he was saying. "Not at all."

"Me neither," said a beefy woman, his wife as I figured.

Cleon nodded. "I saw the whole thing, from beginning to end. They did it all in cold blood."

The farmer shook his head, sympathetic. "I never had no luck with speculators. You see that rig outside?" He pointed out the window with his shoulder and I looked—sure enough, the house was standing among barren hills, and on one near the house there were the remains of a well, a stripped derrick, and an engine house left standing because it was cheaper in those days to leave them than tear them down.

"A wildcatter come by a few years ago with leases and things. Gonna make me a rich man, he says—all sorts of promises. He drills two thousand feet down and all he finds is salt water, and that salt water runs down the hill and over the cotton and ruins the soil."

Cleon shook his head. They were all shaking their heads.

"Not that the land was ever much good," the farmer added. "You know what they say about Oklahoma—

the animals are so scrawny, a dog's got to lean up against a fencepost to get enough strength to bark."

That he still expected anyone to laugh at that old joke showed a lot of optimism. Nobody did, except him, which only led him to try again.

"They also say about Oklahoma that it takes three quail to say one bobwhite."

Cleon looked at the tablecloth and smiled a little. The farmer's wife picked up some needlework.

I could tell the farmer was a little put out by the response to his humor. "Well, I don't farm anymore anyhow," he went on. "Work for the railroad," and he looked down at a pocket watch, as if to prove it.

At this point, a man came in from the rear of the house, a doctor by his bag and black cutaway. Cleon stood in a hurry.

"How is she?"

"She swallowed a lot of water. It ain't pneumonia, but it's like it. I gave her some drops–about all I can do. Try and feed her some soup, unless she chucks it up."

The wife said she would–the farmer clucked his tongue and got up, fetching a cap and lunchpail.

"What about the fever?" asked Cleon.

The doctor pointed at the Peruna bottle in my hand. "That's about as good as anything," he said, and then came over and took a good slug himself. I was about to say, what about me, but the doctor must have read my mind, because he looked down and simply said, "You'll heal," which I guess he figured was all I was worth of his vast training.

"Who did this, anyway?"

"Pan-Oklahoma," Cleon answered.

The doctor nodded, as if he should have known, and shook hands all around, making his goodbyes.

"I'll walk you out, doc," said the farmer, then looked over at Cleon and me. "Just stay clear of those people from now on." With that advice, he took the doctor's arm and they left. Cleon vanished into the back of the house, where Lena apparently was.

It was only now that I began to wonder what Cleon was doing there, and the natural question that followed —what I was? There was only one answer, and that was he'd followed us after our capture. The gunshots on the dome had woken him—he'd hidden back in the trees and when the Hellmen had brought the three of us down the hill and thrown us in the van and moved out, he had followed, that not being so difficult, a car not being able to make much better time than a buggy over back roads in a storm, and then had had the unique experience of, as he'd said, seeing it all happen, crouching in the blackjack watching six grown men kick the stuffing out of his daughter, and then my fight with the Hellmen that followed. Having witnessed my fight, that meant he'd seen what went before it, mainly my powwow with Hellman, but whether he knew the subject of that meeting I couldn't tell. At least he'd gotten me the best treatment possible, having waited till morning and then come out from cover, loaded the living onto the buckboard and traveled down empty roads until a farmhouse turned up, with a doctor near at hand.

And now he was in a back bedroom with his daughter

who, if she had something like pneumonia, was probably dying, medicine being what it was then. That seemed a waste of life to me but perhaps was to be expected when your stupid lady pighead took you down paths you had no business traveling. I couldn't pity her much, no matter what her shape, because she'd gotten what she'd deserved. The same with Cleon—I couldn't pity him because he'd never done anything to stop her. You might say that left me with plenty of opportunity to pity myself, but I didn't, having learned long before that were I to take the time to feel sorry for my mistakes, I'd never get up in the morning. No, on my part it was a business loss, a speculation gone bust and nothing more. The sick wouldn't get any better for my sympathy and besides, I had my own problems.

What I mostly did that day was sleep. When I woke again, it was dark outside and the room stank from kerosene lamps. On top of the pain, I felt a new something pressing inside me, down in the gut, so I struggled to my feet, wrapped my shirt tight around my waist, and staggered into the kitchen.

The wife was there, stirring something on a wood stove. She asked how I was faring—I grunted some answer and asked how you got out in back.

She knew what I was talking about. "Down to the end of the hall—the door on the right."

I hobbled past and down the hall, wincing every time

foot hit floor. There were three doors at the end, left, right, and center, and it isn't surprising in my condition that I chose the wrong one, the left one, and so instead of the sight of a dark backyard and an outhouse on a mound, I found myself in a bedroom lit by one low lamp, with Lena on her back beneath a pile of quilts on an iron bed and Cleon curled up in a chair directly beside her, holding her hand.

It was two surprises at once really, the first surprise being there at all and the second, the surprise of seeing her the way she was, washed and dressed by the wife, I imagine, as best she could, with her hair combed and fanning out on the pillow and a frilly gown on, but her face very pale, except where it was purple from bruises, and her eyes still black. Her knees were drawn up and she was shivering so much, the bed sang.

Cleon saw me and put his finger to his lips, shushing.

"I was looking for the crapper," I whispered back.

He put his finger to his lips again.

At that point, the bed started to creak loud. Lena was doing it—it was like a spasm had hit her, the way she curled in tighter on herself, clutching herself, sobbing, twisting, and jerking this way and that under all those covers. Cleon felt her forehead.

"It's the chills again—she's burning up."

He tried to rearrange the blankets and make the pile thicker, but there wasn't much he could do. There was panic in his eyes, and he looked helplessly around the room. Then he spotted me, and even though we'd just spoken, he seemed shocked to find me there.

"She's burning up—you can feel it," he repeated.

"Maybe more blankets," I said, just guessing.

"I got every one in the house."

At that she cried out loud and said something. Her tongue was thick and I couldn't make it out. Delirium, I figured, and so did Cleon, turning as white as she was.

"Could you go look again?" he begged.

I turned and ran up the hall in my shirt. The wife was still in the kitchen.

"He needs more blankets."

"There ain't no more—I swear it. She gonna die?"

I was in no mood to shoot the shit with her, so I hurried past, into the living room. Just as Cleon had said, everything was stripped, even the rug off the floor. I looked everywhere and found nothing—passing through the kitchen, the wife was gone, and since I didn't want to come back empty-handed, I took a couple of towels and the cloth off the table, just to show I'd tried.

When I got down the hall again, the wife was there, ear up against the door. I made to push past her but she stopped me.

"I don't know that you should just now."

Puzzled by that, I leaned against the door and listened myself.

I could hear Lena—it wasn't hard as she was practically shouting. She was saying the same thing over and over, although I could only guess at the meaning—"No, no . . . no, Richard . . . don't, please . . . no, no . . . please don't . . . please," or words to that effect.

In between her cries I could hear Cleon trying to soothe her down, but with not much confidence in his voice.

Then he left off and as I assumed, gave up trying, leaving her to go on about Richard, whoever he was. Then we heard the bed creak loudly as if somebody was jumping on it. In a minute, Lena's shouts began to diminish, and although she kept calling out to Richard, it was in a softer, more distant tone.

"What ought we to do?" That was the wife beside me.

"I got no idea."

I suspect she was moved more by curiosity than by good will, and I stopped her hand from the doorknob. After a moment though, it occurred to me she might be right, since Cleon could be in need or Lena dead, so I allowed her to open the door.

Well, what I saw, I'd seen before, in tough times on cold nights between men and men, but this was the first time I'd seen it between a man and his daughter. What Cleon had done was strip down to his skin, throw off the covers, and climb in bed beside her, curling his arms and legs around her and nesting up next to her from behind, giving her all he had left to give, namely the heat of his own blood. Lena, of course, was too delirious to know this—she was trying in a feeble way to pry his hands loose from around her waist, still talking to Richard but confusing him with her father, and moaning, ". . . please, Richard . . . no, please . . . don't touch me . . . please, don't hurt me," and so on.

At that point Cleon began to cry. That old man just

buried his face in her hair and sobbed into it, bawling like a baby. How many Richards had been in her life he couldn't know, but one was enough to bring him to tears.

The wife was highly interested—I had to use both hands to pull her away from the crack in the door.

8

It could very well be Cleon's device turned the trick, for by the next morning, the fever had broke and Lena was resting at ease, although none too conscious and by no means out of danger. The doctor dropped by for lunch and checked her over again, saying the usual about how he was just an assistant to the Great Healer who cures and kills according to his own designs, an excuse for shortcomings few of us other mortals are granted, wrapped my back again, and left with three bucks of Cleon's, saying all we needed now was rest.

Well, I hated to rest, have always hated to rest, and it's the final practical joke of somebody whose sense of humor I have never cottoned to that I have been condemned to rest for the remainder of my days here at what they call a home, though you could hardly tell, what with the food and the forms. It seems one of the papers I signed on coming here authorizes the government of the United States to take away various parts of my body when it gets the urge, because that's what the doctors here have been doing for the last five years without one word of explanation, so far having separated me from my spleen, one kidney, and one lung. I can only guess the Army wants to know how little a man needs left inside him to still soldier and I'm convinced they won't be satisfied until they relieve me of my heart and my stomach. Perhaps they're trying to put an end to goldbricking—perhaps in some future war, only death will get you sent to the rear, not a wound, with some three-rocker sergeant bawling, "No intestine? That ain't no excuse. You can pull a trigger with no intestine," in which case I will be to blame, and to all future generations of doughboys, I make my apologies in advance.

What made this rest cure even more irritating was that I wanted with all my heart to be gone and away from those two, even though my body couldn't accomplish it. I wished them well enough, but hanging around with Cleon and Lena was simply embarrassing, what with her just limp in her bedroom, black and blue all over like spoiled fruit, and him padding around the house with soulful eyes, glancing at me now and then and sighing loud enough to move the curtains. And the amusements in that place were few—the wife was about as desirable as the stews she cooked—you could look at the colored plates in the big Bible or the pictures of all the relatives in Wichita Falls, most of them horsy young girls peeking out from behind some bogus studio arbor in the family album, for just so long before your skin started to crawl. It was the shits—I'd tried my try, the job was over, the episode finished, and I wanted to be gone; and to have the three of us still forced together was uncomfortable and in plain bad taste.

Two mornings later, however, I awoke from the settee with some numbness where the pain had been, which I took as a good sign, meaning things were knitting finally, and given a good breakfast, I believed I might even be able to move on that day. I was in the process of feeling myself up and down and considering my chances when Cleon came down the hall from the back, excited. He said Lena had been opening her eyes and then dozing off again all morning, but it looked like she was finally coming to. With that, he went back, figuring I'd follow him. I didn't care to especially, but I did anyway, I suppose wanting, before I left, the satisfaction of seeing Lena helpless and for once well knowing it. When I reached the back bedroom, Cleon was in his usual chair and he'd brought another one over to the bed for me.

She looked a lot better. In fact, she looked pretty good—I'd never seen her face in its best light, since at the dome it had always been decorated with grease and mud, and since we'd been here, it had been swollen twice its normal size, but now it had shrunk back to what you could call basic Lena and it turned out it was a pretty good face for a woman, what with round eyes and nice full lips. Relaxed there, sunk into that down pillow, her neck showing and her arms stretched out, I got the first indication of her true age, which was around twenty-seven, since I could now easily see she had the face of a twenty-seven-year-old girl, one you might see selling gloves behind some counter or doing handwork in some backyard under a shade tree. Her eyes fluttered and opened, then shut again.

"Lena? Lena, honey?" Cleon whispered.

She murmured something and brushed away some hair from her face. Cleon touched her forehead with a hesitant hand.

"She's a lot cooler now," he said, and brought his mouth down to her ear. "Lena—you hear me?"

Her eyes opened. She mumbled something again—Cleon picked up a pitcher of water off the bedstand and poured her a full glass, which she quickly downed with his help. When she finished, Cleon lay her back on her pillow and returned smartly to his seat.

Her eyes opened once more—she looked over at Cleon, then at me, with wonder on her face. You could tell she was having a hard time putting it all together.

"Where did you come from?" she whispered to Cleon.

"I followed you from the dome, Lena. You've been real sick, but you're okay now."

She looked around the room again. This time, when

she saw Cleon her eyes narrowed. All of a sudden she sat bolt upright.

"What the hell are you doing here?" she croaked.

Both our mouths dropped open. Neither of us could believe her. "Jesus, lady," I said. "He saved your life."

But Cleon wouldn't take it personally. He gently forced her back down again. "It's okay, Lena. We're with decent people."

She lay still for a second. "Hellman," she said, and you could see it all coming back. Gasping, "I've got to go," she sprang up again. This time Cleon was there to hold her—she twisted in his arms, yelling and cursing him, but then began to choke and cough, a cough she couldn't control that sapped her strength so she had to fall back, snatching at the covers and hacking into the pillow.

"Don't you think you ought to take it easy?" I said.

She was weak—she knew it, to my pleasure, and being so weak scared her. But Lena, when she was scared, was the sort to attack—in this case, she rolled around in bed and turned her guns on me.

"Where's Jimmy?"

"They hung him. They could have hung you, too."

"You were supposed to be on watch," she snapped.

I still couldn't believe her. She was rising from the grave to take depositions. Cleon was waving his hands and shushing her.

"Lena, now you been sick . . ."

"It was raining," I shouted past his shoulder as he rose to come between us.

"It always rains," she screamed back, her voice suddenly fully healed.

"You think this was my fault?"

"Now don't provoke her . . ." Cleon begged.

But I was the one provoked. I was damn mad, mad I'd come into this room, mad I'd ever used up one ounce of interest on this silly ginch badmouthing me on her back, so I shoved Cleon aside ("Let's not get excited," he was whining), ripped open my shirt, tore all the bandages away, and shoved a chest full of nice rusty red scabs in her face.

"How do you think I got these, Lady," I bellowed. "Shaving?"

She took a deep breath. "You tell me how you shave!" she bellowed back.

"Both of you! Both of you!" Cleon was shouting, trying to get between us again, figuring at least one of us was going for the other, but before I could touch her, Nature provided the remedy, since her last bellow had snapped the string and she suddenly turned beet purple, her mouth formed an O, and she began to cough again, out of control, hacking over and over as she tried to catch her breath, but the vicious cough prevented it, and she pounded the bed feebly with her hands. Her tongue suddenly clicked against the back of her throat—she doubled up over the side, hands groping for a bedpan that lay there, but too late—before she could grab it, her body gave one big twitch and with a roar, she puked all over the rug.

"There's the soup," I said quietly. Feeling vindicated, I turned on my heel and stomped out, leaving them to each other. Down the hall, I passed the wife, who had heard the fracas and looked worried, but I only said, "The soup," and continued onto the porch.

I stomped pounding up and down that plank porch for a long while, letting my rage steam out through my nostrils. Fortunate for her she'd puked, I said to myself, because one second more and her bruises would have made a reappearance, and screw all that crap about the fair sex, because she had been unfair to me from the beginning and never more unfair than just then, and the only fair thing to do to someone who called you a coward was to spoil the teeth that had spoken that lie, at least the way I understood things.

As my anger cooled, I realized Cleon had joined me on the porch some time ago and, in fact, was pacing back and forth as I was, bumping shoulders sometimes with me when we crossed in the middle. I said nothing to him, thinking no more of his company than hers. It was occurring to me that my legs were feeling pretty good after all, that my back didn't hurt nearly so bad as earlier in the morning, and that in fact there was no reason I couldn't leave right then and there. So I stopped Cleon with my hand and looked in his face.

"She's crazy," I said. "You must know that by now. I'd guess there are still things that can be done for her." Without waiting for his answer, I ducked into the house and gathered up my gear.

When I came outside again, Cleon had slumped into a broken-down rocking chair. I sat on the steps nearby and began to tug my boots on.

The sight of him sitting there like a stunned sheep

rekindled my anger. "And you're no better. You just sit there and take it!"

"I know I do! I owe it to her, that's why," he answered, with some strength in his voice.

Sure, sure, I nodded, not wanting to waste time arguing with him. But even pretending to listen was a mistake, because he took it as a sign to continue.

"Her ma was the same way. The same way. A temper and a bad mouth." He sucked in his cheeks. "I was new to the country—I thought all American women were like that."

I wasn't listening—I was getting dressed.

"I figured a kid might help bring us together," he went on. "People told me that happened. Not this time though—not with Rachel. When Lena was born, I was out of the picture, just like that. Rachel had what she wanted and I could go to hell—I only had to touch that kid and she'd go out of her mind, yelling at me."

He thought for a while and sighed. "So I run off."

"Of course you run off." I was fed up with his whining. "What else could you do?"

With that, he suddenly shook a finger at me in a feisty way. "You're wrong! You're one hundred percent wrong! That kid was mine, too—I had a right to her just as much as the mother did. You're wrong—I know that now. I should have stayed and fought for her, toe to toe. No woman should have run me off." And he looked prepared to back his words with his veiny old fists.

"You're crazy too," I said simply, having only at that moment realized it.

"The hell I am. I ain't crazy—I'm right." His gray hair was flying as he shook his head. "And I'm going to fight for Lena. Just like Rachel—she don't want me either, but I want her and this time I'm staying, no matter what she does."

I just stared at him.

"You don't understand, do you?" he said.

"Not really."

"Well, maybe I didn't explain it right." He sank back into his chair. "You couldn't be expected to understand anyway, could you? You don't know the first thing about it."

Time to leave, time to leave, I thought to myself, and stood to do it.

"And you're just going, like that?"

"Just like how?"

"You're going to let them get away with what they done to you?"

"You asshole," I shouted. "You never get back at anybody. Don't you know that yet?"

Well, that little meanness on my part seemed to wash some of the sand out of him. He sighed again and pulled off his boot, took from it his roll and began to count off some bills.

"I don't think you did much. But I thank you for what you tried." He held out a handful.

I eyed the money—perhaps twenty-five bucks there. Sure I could have used them, but not right then, not from the mad daddy of a mad lady, not from somebody I held in such low regard. I shook my head and said, "I'm okay."

He shrugged and stuck out his hand. "Well, all right, then. Shake, anyway."

I thought it over and then shook the hand, hoisted my gear, and walked off, heading for the picket fence that surrounded the farmhouse and the road I could see stretching beyond. Were my ears perking—was I listening with every step for a voice to hail me, to call me back, to beg forgiveness, to press the money on me again? No fucking way. At that moment, my heart was going in the same direction as my feet, only faster.

But I do admit that once past the fence, I looked back over my shoulder. Cleon had left the porch—he was ambling sadly around the side of the house, toward the hill to one side where the derrick stood. As I moved away, I saw him struggle up half the slope, turn and sit heavily there, just mooning and looking down on the house, on Lena's bedroom window, sitting there in the derrick's shadow.

9

That I eventually got back together again with Lena will come as no surprise—anybody who knows at all what happened at Apache Dome knows what's gone before were just the preliminaries, but I don't want to give the impression that I returned in the same direct, one foot ahead of the other, fashion in which I left. Maybe our reunion was in the cards, but there were some things to get out of the way. You put two people together in a dark room and they're bound to stumble together sooner or later, but they'll spend some time bouncing off the walls and tripping over the furniture first.

One thing I've noticed about women over the years is that they'll tease you and hump you and give you a different set of rules every morning until you commence to stand up for yourself, at which point they'll holler cop and try and get you arrested as a pervert. This is certainly what Lena did regarding Pan-Oklahoma—after having given the fig in every way possible to that company, all she could think of to do after the battle was lost was to drive to Ringling and file a complaint with the county sheriff. And according to Cleon, who was there, she actually expected that to be enough, that the law would give her satisfaction, something she probably learned in some red schoolhouse somewhere and to me is a perfect argument for sending children out to work when they are seven or so, since for me, education is the first of many sorrows we endure in our lives, in that the more you learn, the more you suffer.

The sheriff at that time was a man named Voorhees who had been elected unopposed for years, mostly due to a resemblance to the late President McKinley. I saw him dedicate a sewer once and can testify to his ability with words, since he only used long ones that rolled out of his mouth like tapeworms, and it was he, in his splendid office in the courthouse, to whom Lena poured out her tale of woe.

Cleon said he listened to it all intently, with his finger laid alongside his nose. When she finished, he considered and then slowly answered, "That is the most brazen act of brigandage I have ever heard."

Finding him so much in agreement, Lena demanded he take a crew of deputies out to the property and kick Pan-Okie off. Voorhees thought some more and then shook his head.

"No, Miss Doyle—that is not good enough for me."

Lena began to jump up and down about how it was plenty good enough for her, but he stopped her with his hand. No, he went on—it wasn't enough just to disperse the scoundrels. They'd only return when the law left. No—she shouldn't underestimate her power as a citizen and a defendant. And what was his solution?

A federal injunction.

How I wish I could have been there.

To her credit, Lena at this point realized she was being diddled, but Cleon quieted her and held her from leaving, hoping against hope there might be something in what Voorhees was saying. But he was just double-talking away, off on his own, going on about proper procedures and licensed attorneys, cease and desist, and so on.

Cleon himself was losing hope—he glanced over at Lena and noticed she was staring at a picture hanging on a nearby wall, one of a collection of photos and souvenirs and medals and such that some men fancy. And when he looked closely at it, he saw it was taken at a banquet in some hall and there were a bunch of grinning men in monkey suits around a dinner table, and one of them was Voorhees, with the biggest grin of all, and behind them on the podium of the stage was a sign reading "Association of Petroleum Manufacturers, 1907 Convention, Chicago, Illinois." After that, according to Cleon, it was just a matter of getting Lena out of the sheriff's office before she speared him with the brass point on the top of his own American flag, and so much for that sort of law.

But after she got herself calmed down later, Lena realized there was another sort of law, that there was in fact a group of lawyers in the state who specialized in property suits and antitrust, so firing up her spirits once more, she set out after them. After them is the right phrase—they surely didn't want anything to do with her, having heard of her situation and knowing full well it wasn't worth a pipeful of their time, so she had to chase them literally, Lena running up and down the plank sidewalks of Ringling in the one woman's dress she owned, trying to head them off the way a cowboy corners a steer, the difference being the steer is stupid and doesn't know how to put up an out-to-lunch sign, and those lawyers did. If at this stage in her progress, Lena was losing hope, she sure wasn't letting it show to Cleon, who was forced to puff after her, nosing through the sidewalk traffic and grabbing at his heart while she whooped after her prey ahead.

Her attention gradually centered about a lawyer named Fraines, who dodged her with an ease gained through years of practice. After a week's effort netted her nothing, Lena wised up and decided to lay a trap for him, which she sprung of all places in a cathouse, which shows she lacked sense but not cunning. Cleon told me he never felt more like pulling his coat up over his head and blending with the shadows than he did that evening while they lay in wait in some upstairs hallway, listening to all the giggles and glasses tinkling and the Victrola and all the other sounds of a gentleman of the bar going down on a whore in the inner room.

Finally, about midnight, the Victrola clicked off and there were sounds of leave-taking. The door opened, revealing the lawyer, a short scruffy man in a vest being kissed on the forehead by a gap-toothed girl about a foot and a half taller than him.

"Mr. Fraines, I have some affairs to talk over with you," Lena said when his eyes met hers.

According to Cleon, the lawyer slammed the door on them, opened it again, emerged trying to pull on his coat, red all over, gave Lena a straight-arm, stomped down the hall, stopped, and finally threw his coat on the floor with a mighty oath. Resigned, he motioned them on around a corner in the hallway and sat them both down on a couch.

Lena had the lease out. The lawyer snatched it up and read it over quickly. It wasn't enough, he said—she'd have to check at the courthouse for counterclaims.

Lena told him she had already and it was clear.

The lawyer shrugged. "Then you have a lease."

Cleon said she beamed—that was all she wanted to hear, all she had ever wanted. The land was hers and Pan-Okie had no right to it whatever. Now what did she have to do to get it back?

"Get an injunction," said the lawyer.

Lena's face fell away like a landslide.

"The sheriff told us to get an injunction," said Cleon quickly. "We think he's crooked."

"He is. He's also right."

"All right, then," Lena yelled. "Get me an injunction!"

Cleon said Fraines only chuckled. "And what if I do? What Pan-Oklahoma does then is file a countersuit. They'll find something in that—there's always something in a lease—and the case will go to the courts. Do you know what follows?"

"Of course I do," Lena answered, convincing nobody, so the lawyer continued.

"The courts will delay, is what—extensions, motions, postponements. Changes of venue. Mistrials. Your case will bounce over here and roll over there and get lost and get found, and then one day, out of the clear blue, pop—you'll get your injunction."

Cleon said he could tell by his tone they still weren't supposed to be happy.

"Of course, that will all take three to five years and by then they'll have pumped every barrel your land has to give."

Lena was dumbfounded. And all of a sudden out of her league, just as I had been with her. All she could do, according to Cleon, was whisper, "How can they do that?"

"How can they do that?" the lawyer boomed. For good measure he shouted it again, until doors in the hallway started banging open. "My God, lady—they own the courts! Where the hell have you people been?"

Cleon says he tried to exit at this point, figuring they'd wasted enough of the man's time, but Lena was limp and wouldn't budge. "We heard you were against the trusts," she said, almost too soft to hear.

"When it suits me. Look, you people can't afford me anyway. You fight them to the finish and you'll have to spend so much on legal costs, you'll wind up using every dime from your settlement to pay my fee. That's why nobody holds out against Pan-Oklahoma, lady. They've got you—and you'll excuse the expression—by the short hairs."

Lena just sat there in a lonely heap, like something boned by a butcher, sensing for the first time she was licked.

"Take what they'll give you," the lawyer added. "That's my best advice."

But he must have taken pity on her, because as he started to get up, he paused.

"The only other thing I can see you doing, and I say this knowing full well to whom I'm speaking, is find some men and get it back yourselves."

Lena only snorted.

"By force?" asked Cleon.

"I'll deny I ever said it," said the lawyer. "But if you've got a taste for it, you can cut up those men out there into little cubes and nobody can say it's any more than self-defense."

"And how are we supposed to do that?" Lena sighed.

But that was as far as the lawyer was going to go. With a shrug, he stood up, straightened his tie, checked himself in the mirror on the wall, and walked away. When he got to the stairs he turned back once more.

"And if you try to see me again, I'll swear out a warrant against you."

And with that fare-thee-well, he was gone.

I knew none of this at the time, being not that distant in miles but long gone in heart and mind. Having, as I said, written off my time at Apache Dome as a business loss, I was eager to have a business gain next. To that purpose, I'd fallen in with a bunch of speculators, some of whom I'd had a nodding acquaintance with over the years, and entered into a partnership I felt would prove profitable.

The deal concerned a manufacturing plant newly built in some fields a few miles out of Ringling, sitting by itself all brick and cast iron in the middle of the prairie like a cavalry fort, its only visible connection with civilization an electric trolley line. In those days, the trolley companies were very powerful—not many people knew it but the companies themselves were heavily into real-estate development, which took the form of buying up large tracts of worthless land somewhere near a city under the name of some phony company, subdividing it and laying out lots and streets and schools, printing expensive rotogravure brochures about how Dinktown or whatever was the most modern, clean, up-to-date new neighborhood for residence and industry around, as warranted by the fact that the so-and-so trolley company had felt it worthwhile to gamble building a line out to it even before it came into existence. So everybody would buy lots, figuring the trolley company knew something they didn't, which was in its own way true, because the trolley company knew it could make a bundle just on the nickel fares the crowds would pay to take a look at the property. In those days, the trolley companies were lessons to us all.

As for this plant, we of course had no notions of leasing or buying it—I will have failed in every way to acquaint you with the life I led if you figure we wanted to do anything but rob it, which seemed a good idea, since it was so off by itself, and since it met its payroll regularly every Friday.

The plan was simple—two of our number got hired on and come one late Friday afternoon cold-cocked the company guard at the iron gate and let the rest of us in. While I and some others held the drop on the workers in the payline, the rest stormed into the payroll office and started shoving the bills into valises. I was feeling confident of success, standing there with my bandana over my nose, but then from the office came three shots and with that, a deadly crossfire began from a crowd of bulls concealed across the yard. It was clear somebody had talked and we were well expected.

The trouble with these sorts of ventures was that the partners were only linked by greed and nothing more honorable, and when that urge was blocked, the partnership dissolved, as it did at that minute, every man suddenly an independent contractor and running for his life, with myself, who had hoped for success but planned for failure, not far from the lead. Ducking bullets, the others leaped on their ponies or piled in the one car we had—I chose another way, sprinting down the trolley line, off across the vast dry fields, and finding a long winding gully, jumping to the bottom and racing away down it, my chest pinching, those damn boots making hash of my feet, until it was dark and quiet and I was safely alone and nowhere.

I was miserable that night as I lay on my back on the dark prairie, listening to the groundhogs and the snakes. I was up against it—my own schemes had fallen through and I'd done no better trusting to others. It was no longer a question of Mexico—now it was a question of breakfast, and while I still had Cleon's money in the bank, something told me to leave it there and save it for something more important than victuals. Saying that, I was left with only one alternative, which was a job, any job, the first I could find. And the best place for that, no matter how close it put me to the law or to someone who might tie me into the holdup, was town.

And that is how Cleon, Lena, and I came together once more, me on a county road gang slopping asphalt on a dirt street with a mop one day in Ringling, him and her gliding past me down the sidewalk, both of them with their arms full of books, she seeing me full well but not giving me the least time of day, him pausing to greet me with a little secret wave of the hand before he ran after her to catch up.

10

As I suspected he would, Cleon looked me up the next day. At lunchtime as I was fingering the small change in my pocket, there he came, shuffling toward me in his fashion and motioning me away from the gang toward a tree that spread some shade by the roadside. To say he bought me off my principles cheap with a ham sandwich and bottle of beer might be too harsh, but then again might not—survival has a way of cutting through the shit.

He found it hard to get to the subject I knew he'd come with, so for a while we only chatted about the weather and watched the traffic roll past. But after some time, this began to grate on me, since they never gave you much of a lunch hour on these jobs and I could see mine was ending without Cleon getting to that subject, it obviously being Lena, which meant he'd probably drift back tomorrow and if he still couldn't get to it, these noon meetings might go on for the rest of our lives. So, angry that I had to, I brought the subject up.

"Well, what about her?"

He pretended to be at a loss for a while. "Huh? Oh—you mean Lena. Fine, thank you—much better. She's had a small cold lately."

"Well?"

"What?"

"Oh fuck—what's she doing?"

"Well, she's got her business to take care of, things of that sort . . ." And he would have droned on like that had I not punched him in the shoulder to wake him up. He took on a sheepish look.

"It don't appear that good," he admitted, telling me about the sheriff and the lawyer. "There's still some lawyers she hasn't got to, and maybe one of them will take her on for a big cut. If that don't work, she's bought herself a bunch of lawbooks—her feeling is she can teach herself what she needs to know anyway."

I snorted. "You know what I say to that?"

"What?"

But from my expression, he could tell. He nodded and wrung his hands. "Yeah—I suppose I say it too." He paused. "She staked everything on that well. It's sad."

"So?"

"No, I know," he added quickly. "I ain't asking you for anything."

"Then why did you come?"

"No reason." He looked away. "There ain't really anybody else around who'll talk to me."

The poor old bastard. I'd seen his kind at carnivals, the guy they pay to put on a clown face and stick his head through a sheet so people can throw bean-bags at it. Maybe I felt something for him, but then so what? I couldn't help him.

"Anyway, I'm heading off to Mexico," I said.

"I didn't know that."

"Well, I am. Pretty soon."

"I've never been there. I hear it's nice."

I could see the foreman of the crew looking over at me—the other men in the crew were standing and stretching, heading for their tar pots.

"And you're still sticking with her. Thick and thin?"

He shrugged.

"All the way? Even charging up that hill, six-guns blazing?"

He got an uneasy smile on his face. "It does sound awful strange, don't it?"

I saw the foreman pointing at me—he was getting pissed. And I realized, at that moment, so was I.

"Jesus, what's the matter with her anyway," I yelled at Cleon. "They're offering her good money. I'd take it. Anybody else would." I kicked at a rock. "She's some little kid, you know that? She wants the whole goddamn birthday cake and she's going to hold her breath until she gets it!"

Cleon only shook his head, without one word of reply.

You can't avoid people in a small town, so it's not surprising that despite my best efforts, I ran into them again, this time at the town park that weekend. It wasn't much of a park—it was more a vacant lot in the center of town than anything, barren and noisy since the trolleys and freight wagons circled it night and day, but it served as a gathering place for the well-to-do to rest a while and read their papers, and for the less fortunate to retrieve those papers from the trash cans, not only for reading matter but for shoe liners and blankets. That's how I'd gotten the paper at that moment in my hands, and while I sat perusing it, at ease and doing no one harm, I heard a commotion and peered over the top of the page.

There they blew again, father and daughter, this time hollering down one of the gravel paths after a portly, prosperous-looking gentleman with eyes locked forward. Imagine the fix of the poor fellow, accustomed as he was to the same bench at the same calm hour every day, and here this horsefly buzzing and biting from every direction. He unfolded his paper as he sat and tried to hold it up like a wall, but that did no good since Lena was pulling it down with one hand and shoving some notes over it with the other. The horsefly idea must have come to him as well, because at this point, he snatched his paper and rolled it into a tube and began swatting at Lena as she closed.

I wasn't the only onlooker—by now, the entire park was watching this spectacle, maybe fifty men from every level of life joined in the pleasure of seeing a woman make an ass of herself in public view. They hooted and called out advice, but Lena ignored them all, trying to outshout the prosperous man, who was swatting and shouting back, red all down his face and neck, and it finally took all of Cleon's strength and something like a wrestling hold to pull her off him. Her fire sputtered one last curse and then went out, and she let Cleon guide her off through a gauntlet of jolly men who, from their benches on either side, added their comments and observations according to their own sense of humor.

Oh the jokes were flying—in fact, of all the men they passed, I would say I was the only one, hiding behind my paper as I was, who said nothing at all. I was played out—there wasn't anything left to add to what I'd told them already, and there was all of a sudden for me no further satisfaction in laughing at her. I just wanted her to stop, to give up, to go somewhere else, because, by Christ, she was no longer a joke but an embarrassment to me. By that, I mean I was beginning to feel sorry for her too, with the notion that maybe she'd taken more bad from life than she'd spread, and if that was so, if I was feeling some small something for her and her plight, what was I doing behind that newspaper while all around me the male population of Ringling got its rocks off on her as she passed by?

For the next few days I pondered that question in a funk, having nothing but bad words for my pals on the road crew, and no solace but that from the whiskey I bought. I knew I was troubled by what Lena was doing, but not exactly why, although I know I was coming to the conclusion it was time somebody set her permanently straight, not only in her own best interests but the best interests of everyone else. She was not only hurting herself but the town as well, disturbing what people were used to, such as when you won and when you lost, when you spoke up and when you just kept still and took it. In the name of important things—Prosperity, Tranquillity—she had to be educated. After mulling it over, it became clear if I expected that to happen, I among everybody was the most qualified to see it did.

When I finally set out, I went with no plan but at least plenty to say. Tracing her wasn't hard—she spent her days at the courthouse in the law library, pouring over those books of hers. And oh how she stood out there, the one woman in a room of men, drillers, buyers, speculators, all talking in low tones about their million-barrel deals, what they had done, what they could, winking and poking at each other the way men do.

I studied her for a while from the doorway, and when she got up from her books to move to the main desk, I strolled in and sat down across the table from where she was. Cleon naturally was there and his eyebrows rose when he saw me, but he said nothing and there I waited, like a man just resting his feet on the way to somewhere else.

She returned, spotting me, but as on the street, she made no sign. That was fine with me—in my role as invisible man, I reached across the table and snatched away the legal pad she was writing on, and while she paused there with her pen suspended over nothing, looked it over. It had some notes but mostly scribbles, stars and squares and wiggly lines, the things you draw when you're bored, and here and there with heavy boxes drawn around them, the words "Apache Dome." She remained poised, pen in her hand, until I finished reading and put the pad back, at which point she began to write again as though nothing had happened.

"I got something to tell you," I said finally and quietly, it being a library, "You want to step outside?"

She hissed at me to be quiet without taking her eyes off her work.

"I tried to make a deal with Hellman," I said, louder, so she'd full well hear it. "That's how much I was on your side. I was going to sell out and leave you flat. You ask your pa—he was watching."

She didn't twitch a muscle.

"I sure did," I went on, just as loud. "And anybody else would have done the same. And anybody in the future will screw you just as bad, so why don't you give up and forget all this horseshit?"

She still wouldn't look up. I saw her scheme now—there were murmurs around me as those in the room let their conversations slide and turned to listen to me, and she was counting on those murmurs to shame me and make me shut up. But I didn't care—there was nothing I was saying I wouldn't want any man in the room to know, so the next time I spoke, I did it even louder, and for the benefit of all.

"Who do you think you are, anyway? You can't do nothing on your own and you can't trust a soul. Everybody's out for a piece for themselves, including you, including me, including every man in this room and if you don't have the muscle and the brains to pull it off yourself, you're going to get run over. You're weak and dumb—you're a crusty woman with a pig head and nothing more to recommend you, so just where do you get off thinking you, of all people, can lick Pan-Oklahoma?"

I heard voices telling me to pipe down but I paid them no heed, staring Lena right at the point of her head where her eyes would be if she had the nerve to look me in the face. I was ready for her reply, but then what reply—what could she say in her defense? She was furious, I could tell that, pretending to concentrate on her notes but coming to a boil inside.

As usual, I underestimated Lena by a wide mark. I was ready for a comeback, but not an explosion, which is what happened as she threw the chair back with a crash, leapt up and hollered not only at me but everyone else:

"Of course you want me to give in! Of course my daddy does! Of course every man in this room and every man in town does, because if I, some silly and ignorant woman, lick the almighty Pan-Oklahoma, then that makes all of you a pack of gutless, fumbling slugs that don't know your balls from tea bags, don't it?"

I and every other man in that room froze, simply froze. Sitting or standing, frozen in place like a bunny in a car's headlights, each with his mouth hung open big enough to drive a bicycle through.

Oh, Lena!

I don't know how I got out of that room—I can't imagine it was with much style. I seem to remember wandering around town for a while, banging with my fist on walls and pipes just to hear the noise they made, and then it was dark and some city cop was tapping me with his nightstick and asking me to lay off.

I'd handled her all wrong, that was clear, but I couldn't imagine anybody doing it better or any differently. Perhaps it was just the cut of man I was used to running with but the best of us were never at ease in the camp of the opposite sex. I know I've always regarded the most innocent conversation with a woman as one of those telegrams whose message always gets fucked up in the sending, so it isn't surprising Lena and I didn't make contact, despite all my good intentions.

What I couldn't understand, and I gave it a lot of effort, was how after telling her exactly the way things worked, exactly the way the world was run, I still came off looking like a rat. How was that? I was right—of course I was, and what I was telling her was the simple truth all men knew. What magic was there in women that allowed them to turn simple truth around into being chickenshit, which, after all, was the gist of what she'd accused me of. That was the mystery I pondered in those late hours, making use of whichever saloons crossed my path to help me think.

After about half a bottle's worth, ideas began to come. It had something to do with conviction, I suspected. I had always connected conviction with stupidity, though being fair, stupidity could on occasion give you strength. For instance, in the famous old tale of David and Goliath—now I always pictured David as this young wise-ass who was new to the game and unbloodied, and in his ignorance carried a big hard-on toward himself, whereas Goliath was like most of us, big and strong maybe but getting on, having lost a few as well as won some, going through life with that wisdom men have. So when he took the field and saw what the Israelites had put up against him, he had to have a moment's pause when he realized it wasn't another Goliath like himself, which would be expected, but just some punk. He'd have to wonder what that punk had that he didn't. And that, of course, was David's strength, that ignorance, that conviction he could take anyone, and Goliath's weakness the suspicion that things being what they were that particular afternoon, what with his fuzzy head from the night before, maybe David could at that.

All right—Lena was David, that was sure. If Goliath was me, and he did seem like me, I could begin to understand why I'd lost every round with her. She was small and ignorant, but sure—I was big and smart, but I never quite believed in that size or intelligence. What I saw as doing the smart thing was taking the good with the bad, while her ignorance told her you only settled for the good and nothing less, even if it finished you. That was her edge on me, on all of us.

I went that far and then took time out for a few more shots. When I came back to the subject, Lena was looking better and I was looking worse in leaps and bounds. Sure I was smart, but where had it all got me, I thought? Sure I'd gone through a lifetime of pain and privation just to get initiated into the brotherhood, but what good were the secrets of being a man if all you could say was they'd fed you poorly and introduced you to some of the scummier levels of society. Yes, my wisdom had kept me alive, but not any sort of life I could brag about—maybe a few years back, I could have consoled myself that things were going to get better if I waited my turn, but time had put the lie to that just by the fact that I was running out of it with no particular improvement. Maybe what was tripping me up was not what Lena had to say, but the fact it was coming from the mouth of a woman.

A woman. Yes, Lena was a woman, and surely a new strain for me, something much different than those things that took a half-hour chattering among themselves to cross a muddy ditch. There was something to say for her kind of woman, nothing that flattering, but something you had to begrudge. On Lena, if you took her stupidity and sort of turned it around on its side, and you twisted to the other side yourself, that stupidity almost began to look good. She stayed a stubborn idiot, but an idiot who believed in something, and if you kind of squinted, she didn't look much worse than all those clever men I knew who believed in nothing.

Of course, all the above is horseshit, in that I was plenty drunk by then and my eyes were all swollen by the cigar smoke that would hover in those places, and whatever thoughts I had kept blending in and out with the tunes the man was plinking on the thumbtacked piano. I'm not back there—I'm here rotting in Dormitory C and everything I've just said is pure guesswork, going not on not what I thought, which I can never completely remember, but what I did subsequently. From those days until now, whenever anyone has asked me why I've done something or another, I've said because it seemed a good idea at the time, and if you were to stop me on the street as I made my way from the honky-tonks to Cleon's shack behind the hotel around two o'clock that morning, I would have said precisely the same thing and nothing more.

I hauled my pants up in front of that shack and pounded on the door. I heard some furniture moving and Lena calling who is it, but I wasn't interested in amenities by then and kicked the door open with my boot.

She stood there with her hair in pins, her nose still red, and her eyes bleary from her sniffles—Cleon, who'd been sleeping in a chair covered by a blanket, was tangled up in it and struggling to get free.

"Here I am," I smiled.

She spun like a spring released on Cleon. "You've been talking to him again!"

"Just the other day, is all . . ." he pleaded.

"WILL YOU TWO SHUT UP," I boomed, at the very top of my lungs.

It took them by surprise, that bellow. Lena looked at me almost afraid.

"You and your man thing!" I shouted. "Jesus, I'm tired of it! It's a lot of hot air anyway—you didn't lose that hill because of any man!"

"Who said I did?" she protested, but I was way past her.

"No—not them either!" And with a sweep of my hand, I knocked a stack of lawbooks off the table onto the floor. "Because you was pigheaded enough to take on an oil trust! And I'll tell you something—you're gonna need a man to take it back because I sure don't see any gun-carrying women lining up behind you!"

By this time, she'd got herself together enough to snicker at me.

"Yes, me! I was in the Army. I fought in Cuba."

"I didn't know that," said Cleon, quietly.

"Well I did, so I got some idea more than you on how to take a goddamn fortified defensive position!" And for good measure, I knocked over another stack of books.

Lena didn't know what to say. By chance, I'd struck her at the right time—her eyes were heavy with sleep and with her cold, her reactions were off.

"In return for my services, I want twenty-five percent of the operation."

That was enough to bring her to. "Not one damn percent!"

"All you do good is talk dirty."

"I'll take you on out of charity."

I was outraged. "Don't you give me no charity!"

"All right, all right. I'm sorry I said that," she said quickly.

She paused and thought for a moment. "Two percent."

I thought for a moment in turn. "All right, then," I said, calmer. "Two percent. I don't care."

She commenced to stretch her eyes as though she might have dreamed all that had just happened. Cleon sat me down, then put some coffee on the wood stove to warm. Lena continued to pace the room, stretching her eyes with her fingers now and blowing her nose, still not quite awake.

Where had all this come from—who had said anything about taking the hill back? Nobody, but at that stage in the game, there wasn't much else left to do when you thought about it. Some things don't have to be mentioned when they're all that's left.

And where had that matter of a plan I'd spoke of come from? That much I knew—something had transpired between those last meditations of mine and my meeting with Lena and Cleon.

I had been at that bar, or some bar, and that particular one was filled with enlisted men in uniform off a troop train that was standing overnight in the railyards. Now leaning at the bar as I was and watching the boys drink and hearing the old songs sung brought back memories, and as those things go, among the memories flowered the germ of a notion. It would take some military assistance, so spotting an old-timer corporal at a table in a corner nursing his drink in a professional way, I picked up my bottle and headed toward him. I intended to come on in a friendly way, but my reflexes weren't up to diplomacy, what with all the liquor, and though I had planned to set the bottle gently down on the table between us, what I did was kick the chair over and accidentally slam the bottle down, which the corporal took as a sign of hostility, but I relaxed him down well enough when I said I'd come to talk about some profitable business.

Yes, still business. I still thought it was.

11

The thing about war is that it's so much fun, and to all those faint hearts who claim it's the ruination of us all and what keeps us from being God's angels here on earth, I say to them, you go off and find something else as pleasurable as traveling to some foreign land where you shoot the natives and bang their women and drink their booze, burn their houses just for a flame for your cigar, whoop and holler with a bunch of good pals, run around stealing things and writing dirty things on walls and playing practical jokes, and all this encouraged and underwritten by your own government—find something just as good and come back and tell us about it, and you stand half a chance, but until you find this other amusement, the rest of us will settle for warring in the meantime.

I say this only to set the tone of what transpired in the second boxcar from the end of the troop train that was preparing to pull out from the railyards the next morning. For, though everything else about the train was frantic and hurried, what with the engineer behind schedule and forcing steam and all those enlisted men in their campaign hats with their Enfields jamming to get on board the three old pullmans, and officers marching up and down the train's length shouting, inside the boxcar was dark, quiet, and very amiable as my partners and I sat talking with two military men and a whiskey bottle was passed around, the early hour notwithstanding.

My partners—my new partners—were of course Lena and her dad, and the military men were Corporal Stapp, my acquaintance of the previous evening, and his good friend in the Quartermasters, Sergeant Treadlo. To show how much Treadlo had warmed to our problem and my notion to deal with it, he'd gone out of his way to draw a little sketch map of the dome, military style, with the landmarks and elevations laid in, and he was showing it to us with the air of a man who takes pride in his craft.

"It's a classic situation," he was saying. "The taking of high ground against superior forces in strong defensive positions. Now I've taken the liberty of preparing some lines of attack, which you can take as suggestions."

Lena took the map and glanced it over with obvious admiration. Treadlo winked at me—I grinned back and passed him the bottle. What fun we were all going to have.

"I haven't had much time to prepare," Treadlo continued, "but I would say all considered, your biggest problem is not taking the dome itself but defending it against the counterattack that will come when the hostiles regroup here at the bottom."

"I don't follow this at all," muttered Cleon.

I haven't yet mentioned that of all of us, he was the only one not in the spirit of the thing. Lena hushed him, but Treadlo waved her away—answering doubts was one of his great pleasures, you could tell.

"Just look at the map, Mr. Holder. You can see what with the terrain, there are any number of blind approaches to the dome you can infiltrate easy enough, especially if you go in Sunday morning as we all suggest . . ."

"Some of them will be sleeping off Saturday night," I stuck in.

"Exactly. And with one of you making a diversion . . ."

"That's where I don't agree," Stapp spoke up. "I don't think it's wise to divide your forces."

"Well, he don't agree," Treadlo replied, "and that's his right, but personally, I think you're going to need something to distract the men on top away from your main force . . ."

"Main force?" Cleon repeated, not believing any of this.

"That's right," Treadlo rolled on, "but that decision is up to you. Anyway, as I said, the squeeze comes when they try to knock the three of you off the top and that's why you need the little something extra we can supply." And with that, he got up off the crate he'd been sitting on, ripped the top off with a prybar, and revealed my plan, namely a case of hand grenades all sitting there cuddled in their excelsior like eggs gone bad in a nest.

At the evil sight of them, Lena gasped. Treadlo, Stapp, and me winked all around. Cleon just eyed them straight and it was a while before I realized he didn't know what they were.

"They're hand grenades."

He went kind of pale.

Treadlo treated him with handsome patience. "Better than dynamite. If the blast don't get them, the steel will."

Cleon reached out and picked one up, letting it roll in his palm, afraid to put his fingers around it. "They're awful heavy," he said.

"That's the nice thing about them," Treadlo answered. "You don't have to throw them—on a hill, you can roll them down. Now there's twenty-five in a case and I think you'd require at least two cases. Right, corporal?"

Stapp nodded. "At least two."

"So—that's fifty of them." Treadlo calculated for a moment. "Say—we'll let them go for, oh—one twenty-five a case. That's two fifty, and we'll throw in the map. What do you say?"

"I say yes," said Lena, convinced. I nodded—it was my idea. Everybody turned to Cleon, who was slowly shaking his head.

But before he could answer, there was the sound of the door latch banging, and Treadlo just managed to get the lid back on the grenades and his ass on the lid before the door swung back, flooding us with sunlight and revealing a shavetail lieutenant looking us all over with some surprise.

"I've been looking for the route chits, Treadlo," he said, after a second's pause.

"Moressy had them last time I saw, lieutenant. You might check with him," Treadlo answered, cool as ice.

The lieutenant looked us over again, turned to go—as he did, Treadlo stopped him. "Oh Lieutenant Truman, these are some friends of mine. Mason here and me served in Cuba together."

Truman looked us over for a third time. Now you knew damn well he was wondering what his quartermaster sergeant was doing in a boxcar getting drunk with three civilians at nine thirty in the morning, but you could also recognize that familiar look on his face which said, what I don't know won't ever, ever hurt me, so he only nodded and said, "Good day to you folks," and even had the manners to shut the boxcar door after him when he left. Treadlo, Stapp, and me winked and giggled at each other all over again—Cleon remained unaffected by the humor and with Truman gone, we all turned back to him.

"Well, what do you say?" Lena asked him.

Cleon shook his head again. "All the plan I see is—you three people go up on that hill and kill everybody."

We all answered at once, Lena because she wanted to

be halfway there already, Treadlo because his effort wasn't being appreciated, and me because, while Cleon was absolutely right in his criticism, it was the only plan we had or ever would, given the circumstances. But none of us got heard and Cleon waved us all down.

"We're using my money, damn it! Ain't there no other way?"

"I was just using what resources you have at hand, Mr. Holder," answered Treadlo, a little peeved. "I wonder what you was expecting."

"Do you want me to say please?" Lena asked, disgusted. "All right then—please, Daddy. Buy them for me . . ."

"Oh quiet, Lena. That ain't it, and you know it," he answered, holding up his hand. He looked torn, sitting there, torn between seeing his daughter get what she wanted and seeing his daughter already dead, which at that moment were the same thing for him.

I nudged her. "Talk to him."

"*You* talk to him," she snapped back.

"He's *your* daddy."

I had her there, much to her displeasure. She sighed, tapped him on the shoulder, and walked off into a dusty corner of the boxcar to wait for him. Cleon hesitated, looking at each of our faces for support but seeing none, finally stood and followed her off. She started in with a mad whisper before he got there and she did most of the talking.

While they argued, Treadlo turned to me in an old-buddy way, passing back the bottle. Pointing to the grenades as I took a swig, I asked, "Where are you going with those things?"

"Colorado," he answered. "Putting down a strike in the mines." He took the bottle back again. "Was you really in Cuba?"

"Sure I was."

"I don't remember you."

That wasn't surprising to me. "I was a hostler. I took care of horses."

"A hostler, eh?" He mulled that over—I hadn't told him I was any other brand of soldier, but what with why I'd come to him, he had just assumed. "A hostler." He reflected for a moment. "Well, just do what I do. Shut your eyes and go," and he made an upward motion with his hand.

I nodded—that was about what I had in mind.

"You know if this is the kind of thing you're moving into, you ought to reenlist," he went on. "We've been going all over . . ." and he would have continued with that stock re-up speech had he not been interrupted by Lena and Cleon returning.

Cleon looked resigned and was fingering his roll. "She wants it, so we'll take them," he sighed. "But all I got is two hundred bucks."

Treadlo's face clouded. "That ain't very close, is it?"

"Take it or leave it," said Lena.

Treadlo didn't say anything. A long moment passed and nobody moved. After all that, all that whiskey and the map and the good will, it looked as if he was prepared to leave it, so with a sigh of my own, I reached into my shirt pocket, took out a wad of thirty-five one dollar bills and threw them down.

"There's thirty-five, Treadlo," I said. "There ain't no more."

He eyed the money—then turned to Stapp and the two sort of talked to each other with their eyebrows. They must have decided in that fashion, because Treadlo at last raked in the cash and got up off the grenades.

"All right," he said. "For such nice folks as you."

Cleon had been watching all this with some surprise. "Where did you get that money," he asked me, sensing it was somehow familiar.

"I had it," is all I answered, finding something else to look at besides his eyes.

12

That meeting in the boxcar seems, by the look of it, a straightforward set of dealings between people of honor, but to be sure, there wasn't a soul there who wasn't lying. Treadlo and Stapp, for instance—Stapp the night before in the bar had quoted me a price of a hundred dollars a case, and at the point Treadlo had given his figure to Lena and Cleon had glanced over to see if I was going to protest, the price increase obviously due to seeing the buyer in the flesh and beholding a desperation that inspired them to greater heights, but I had kept my mouth shut, knowing it was a seller's market. Then Lena and Cleon—yes, two hundred bucks was all they had, but not all their assets because we'd taken the precaution of getting what equipment we needed prior to the meeting, specifically hiring a freight wagon and some more weapons, halfway decent ones this time, including an old twelve-gauge shotgun for Cleon, the barrel of which I cut down from thirty inches to ten with a hacksaw, which meant he was not only assured of hitting anything in front of him, no matter how badly he aimed, but very probably innocent bystanders to his rear.

And what about me, who had gone through such a revelation about my past and my present and who seemed to be, for reasons still hazy, a new man? I was tripping over myself with lies, and not only about where that thirty-five dollars had come from but also, as I had confided to Treadlo, my military experience. Still this fact didn't disturb me greatly—I'd never been in a battle and had maybe only raised my head once or twice from the hoof I was treating to hear the distant popping of some great victory, but I figured I knew as much about fighting as anyone else, since when Treadlo had given me his advice about shutting his eyes and going, he confided in me no secret not known to every other soldier in every other war. And while I truly intended to soldier for Lena and, as I expected in a funny relaxed way, die for her, I can't help thinking that in the back of my mind was the coffee grounds of the original con I had brewed, something like maybe Hellman would come and pay me off again, or maybe everyone would get killed but me and the well would come in and I'd be a millionaire—I don't remember anything specifically, but knowing myself, I can't believe I ever did anything for one reason alone.

Relieving the Army of its property was easy enough, since there was a curve on a grade outside of town, well known to those who hopped freights, the trains had to slow to practically nothing to negotiate, and it was there we waited an hour later as our train passed, pulling the boxcar with its door slid open slowly by and Treadlo and Stapp handing the cases down to us almost as if they were standing still. I believe that old soldier Treadlo actually threw me a salute as the box car receded, but then I couldn't see it well and it might have been a gesture of an entirely different meaning.

At any rate, for better or worse there we were, armed and resolved. That was a Friday—our plan was to hit the dome Sunday, so we were forced to stall a day and a half, full of frustration and boredom, with Lena working herself up to a frenzy, Cleon ever more full of misgivings, and me in the sort of mood where wills get written, but only thinking of it, having nothing at all to bequest.

Dawn Sunday found us shivering concealed among the hills perhaps a half mile from the dome. The low slanting sun was in our favor—a night attack might have been better still but they're tricky things, even with people like the Hellmen who knew what they were doing, whereas were one of my command to screw up and wander off in the dark, we would have been reduced by thirty-three percent. You'll notice I said my command, which it was, the other two consenting to take my orders, although there was no doubt it was still Lena's army.

While they waited, I crept up to the top of a rise for a reconnaissance. Shading my eyes to study the dome, I could see Pan-Okie had indeed moved in and from the look of things wasn't finished, since piles of unopened crates and stacks of fresh equipment were scattered around the top. There was a new corrugated iron shack and they'd done some work on the derrick from what I could see, reinforcing the old tower with wooden gussets and putting in new rig irons—stirrups, bearings, and such—and replacing the weary gas engine on its truck with a more powerful and permanent one. Most important, the derrick was working—they'd finished the rigging Lena had started and begun drilling, actually making an oil well and down at least a hundred feet or so because while I watched, the crew of three ample-looking men in overalls and tin hats drew the tool string from the hole and it took a good minute or so to wind the cable in on its drum. I could spy three more men, guards by the rifles they carried, strolling around the dome top, and down at the base by the wire, a picket of four or five on patrol, their slickers and black derbies well visible even at that distance. All in all, and giving account to men still asleep in the buildings, it meant we had a force of maybe twelve to contend with—simple arithmetic indicated we'd have to take out four of them apiece. It wasn't much of a plan at that.

I scuttled back down the hill and reported what I'd seen. Lena got one of those the-more-there-are-the-more-I-slaughter looks and paced about, saying, "All right, then—all right, then" to herself. Cleon blinked but said nothing, not wanting to parade his terrified voice in front of us. What was worse, he was to be the vanguard, the point of the column—we'd decked him out in a teamster's outfit, leather pants and a broad hat, since his job was to get the grenades onto the dome the simplest way we could devise, namely driving them up in the freight wagon hidden under a load of two-by-fours, pretending the lumber was a shipment for Pan-Okie. I myself may have taken a little more time than necessary studying the map but Treadlo had been just about right with the arrows he'd drawn in. There was no arguing with their direction and nothing remained but to follow them.

As Cleon climbed onto the wagon, I could tell he wanted to say something to Lena by the noises in his throat—something final and loving I suppose, since the occasion seemed right for it—but he couldn't get it out, and Lena did nothing to aid the process, turning away from him with some little embarrassment. As she saw it, none of us were present for her sake anyway—we were just some guys who had joined her fight because the cause was so just. At least that was the feeling she gave us, and it was with that air of things left unsaid and motives confused that our assault began.

I know what happened to Cleon, not because I saw it, since I was far away skirting the rise with Lena and moving in through the weeds on the dome, but because he talked about it so much and so excitedly in the days after. As he and the wagon came out from behind the rise and the dome came into view, Cleon said he was sure his thumping heart would give him away, being so uncontrollably loud, until he realized it was merely the echoing sound of the tool string biting rock under the steady up and down of the walking beam beyond and above him. The dome rose up quickly—he could see a new gate across the road and at the gate a Hellman he recognized as Walker, who stepped forward to halt him with a suspicious look.

"What you got in there?" he asked.

"Shipment for Pan-Okie," Cleon answered. I'd coached him over and over on those words, which were all he was supposed to say, but even at that, he said it took him time to get his throat wet enough to say them.

"On Sunday? What kind of slave outfit you work for?"

Cleon just shrugged, on behalf of his slave outfit. Walker glanced at the load in the wagon in a funny way, then turned to open the gate. At that point a familiar voice rang out:

"What about the invoice, Walker?"

And how familiar it was, since it belonged to none other than Captain Hellman himself, lounging in the back seat of his touring car a few yards off. He opened the door to get a better look at Cleon, at which point Bull jumped out and loped over to the wagon, sniffing the wheels.

We hadn't thought Hellman would be there—I sure hadn't thought to coach Cleon what to say if he was, so Cleon consequently could say nothing at all.

"He wants the invoice," Walker repeated, figuring Cleon hadn't heard. Bull hopped on the wagon bed and after snuffling at the lumber came over and began to lick Cleon—Cleon said his tongue was hot, wet, and smooth.

"The invoice," Walker continued, "for this load."

"He said he was sending it on," croaked Cleon, saying something that came to him.

"Who said that?" asked Hellman.

Cleon was inspired. "The dispatcher! The dispatcher did!"

Hellman's eyes narrowed. Cleon counted his sins to himself—Sunday, no invoice, imaginary dispatcher—while Bull sniffed further. Finally, with an annoyed wave of the hand, Hellman motioned him on and whistled to Bull. While the dog trotted back to the car, Walker swung the gate open and Cleon, having barely the strength left to do it, hitched the team's reins.

But just as the wagon was half through the gate, Hellman roared out again. Cleon stood on the brake. "Yes, sir," he gasped, figuring it was all over.

"You tell that dispatcher to include the invoice next time or I'll have his ass."

Cleon said he nodded until his head was coming loose, shook the reins like crazy, and started up the dome road without looking back.

So now he was behind the lines, but it would be hard

to say whether he was actually the first of us to make contact, since at the same time he was having his problems, we were having ours. The idea was for us to slip under the wire and arrive on top the same time as Cleon, and we were well on our way, being held up momentarily at the fence as Rucker, another Hellman, shuffled by on his beat. He was no special threat—either he had just risen or had not slept for hours, for he passed us with a blank expression and disappeared out of sight around the dome's curve.

With that I moved forward, slithered beneath the wire, and took cover up the slope, motioning Lena to follow. She began, having some difficulty, women as I've said doing physical things usually awkwardly, when I looked over and saw Rucker returning in the same dreamy way, just doing time and walking his patrol. I hissed and motioned Lena back—she saw the danger and tried, but at this point got all caught on the barbs and became more tangled the more she struggled, so that by the time Rucker was near, he couldn't help but spot her. She froze, but it was too late—he cut through the weeds toward her with his rifle muzzle trained.

"Well, well, well . . ." he chuckled, seeing his prize.

"Screw you, Rucker," Lena hissed.

She might have been smarter to lay low when I gave her my signal, but her drawing all that attention to herself actually worked out for the best, since it gave me a chance to get in behind him and swing my rifle stock like a baseball bat at his head. He went down hard, but the stock splintered and broke, which gave me a second's concern until I realized Rucker's weapon was whole and most probably better than mine, so I traded the two. I figured Lena could get herself loose, which she did at length with a heave, a rip of clothing, and a sniff for the look of enjoyment on my face.

"How's your cold?" I smiled.

"Fine—just fine," she muttered, and in fact she looked much better now that she was back on her land.

We made it up to the top in good order and hid below the rim, peering over when we heard no suspicious sounds. Cleon was just reaching the top himself and nodding to one lounging guard, he and the wagon crossed the open area toward the derrick.

Now it was intended he would get the drop on the rig crew with his shotgun and hold them there while we dispatched the rest, something that seemed within his ability. But the thing about making plans, of course, is that the other fellow doesn't know them and does whatever he wants to do in ignorance of your needs. As Cleon guided the team toward the rig, another Hellman and one of the worst, Dullnig, happened to be walking across the area and, feeling charitable, perhaps because it was the day of his Lord, he suggested to Cleon he stack his load over by the rig. Cleon agreed—this was what he wanted to do anyway, but as he veered that way he said he happened to look down and went cold when he saw Dullnig was walking along beside him.

"No, it's all right," he said.

"I'll give you a hand," said Dullnig, unexpectedly friendly for some reason.

"I can ask the boys on the rig."

"They ain't supposed to." He gave Cleon a funny look, wondering why his company was being turned down.

Cleon could only smile weakly—we, from hiding, could see his problem. True, there was the charged shotgun beneath a blanket on the floodboards by his feet, but that was supposedly for the rig crew ahead of him, not Dullnig alongside. He could only rein up by the derrick and sit there totally at a loss. The three drillers looked up, nodded, and went back to work. Dullnig, still in high spirits, rested his rifle against a wagon wheel, pulled out one length of lumber onto his shoulder, and laid it carefully on the ground, starting a pile. At this point, he noticed the teamster wasn't moving.

"I ain't going to do it alone."

We could see Cleon looking at Dullnig and then at the rig crew, knowing if he went for one, the other would jump him and vice versa. And no matter how we cursed him, Lena even more than I, and made twitching motions with our bodies to get him off his ass, he continued to do nothing at all.

Dullnig was likewise peeved at him. He leaned on the wagon side, regarding Cleon with a fishy eye.

"Something wrong with you?"

Cleon shook his head dumbly.

"Then do something."

Our sentiments as well, but words weren't enough—what it took was Dullnig's eyes drifting down onto the load of lumber he alone had been diminishing and seeing, between the boards, something that looked like a crate with something like "Property, U.S. Army," stenciled on it, and looking up at Cleon with surprise and saying something like, "Hey," because just then Cleon scooped up the shotgun, leaped to his feet and, I will swear, with his eyes shut, pulled the trigger.

The proof about the shut eyes was that even with both barrels, he only got Dullnig in the arm, but still the force of the load was enough to spin him around like a top a few times before he fell to the ground, whining and bawling and clutching at his shoulder. The blast spooked the horses, by no means cavalry mounts—they bolted, which sent Cleon, having been standing, over the side and into the dirt, but he managed to roll as he hit and came up with the shotgun on the three stunned drillers, shouting in a cracking voice, "Hands up now . . .!"

I yanked Lena by the shoulder and we came over the ridge at a dead run. The first sound in reply was not a shot but a whistle from below the ridge—Hellman alerted and warning his forces. Dullnig was screaming, flopping around in the dirt—the team was galloping in crazed circles around the rim, looking for an exit. Now some answering fire began from a rifleman across the dome behind some crates. "Cover me," I yelled to Lena as we raced swerving toward the tar-paper shack.

And do you know, for all the piss and vinegar and evil in that woman, her first whiff of battle shook her completely, for she only stood there with her mouth open and a pistol limp in her hand, while about her the bedlam grew. I stopped short, ran back, grabbed her, and with slugs whizzing past, raised that gun arm and pointed her weapon at the far crates like some instructor on a firing range, saying quietly, since I couldn't see shaking her more, "Shoot at them." She nodded, it seeming reasonable, and began a slow fire, accurate enough since she was a good shot. With her in action and Treadlo's advice ringing in my ears, I threw my shoulder to the door and crashed inside the tar-paper shack.

There was a man bare-ass naked at a window peering out through sleepy eyes at the confusion. As he turned, I fired—missed his heart but hit his stomach and saw the blood flowing. I was running, knees high, wading through clothes and boxes and assorted shit on the floor—I saw a man among my feet, rudely awakened and pulling off his blankets, so I threw myself against the wood stove at the room's center. The stove fell over spilling coals on him, and the red-hot piping pitched across his back for good measure. From the way he yowled, I figured I could save his bullet for someone else, and not slowing a bit, I plowed through the door on the far side and out into the crisp morning air once more.

Well, well, well, I remember thinking to myself, standing there and panting. Just that—well, well, well.

I wasn't allowed that luxury long—wood splinters began to fall on me, which meant somebody was shooting up the framing over my head. I crouched down—

the damn horses were masking the firing, galloping madly back and forth with flared nostrils and red eyes, dragging the teetering wagon after but probably not even feeling it as they sought a way out. They finally spotted the road, but racing for it pulled the wagon through a pile of boxes, which sent it up and cartwheeling over, slamming the team to the ground and spilling the remaining lumber and our hand grenades over fifty square yards of area. The horses jerked free from the ripped harness and flew off and away–behind them, I could now see two men, one armed and one not, both sprinting for the cover of the iron shack. Lena was moving toward them to intercept, firing but not hitting anything, what with her running. I raised my pistol with both hands, which is the only way to aim those things, squeezed off a round very carefully, and dropped the unarmed man. The third still sped free and I ran after him, colliding with Lena who was converging on him from the other side and, as I recall, knocked her on her ass, but it was the man who concerned me and by cutting him off I managed to plunge in the door of the iron shack just behind him. Inside, I realized his problem–his handgun was spent and he was going for a rifle on a wall rack, but I had plenty of time and my four shots split his shoulder blades. There was a movement in the corner of my eye, almost behind me–oh dear, I'd fucked myself by advancing too far into the shack and was about to get back-shot myself, but when I turned, it was the sound and sight of a window shattered and the bare ass of another sleeper crashing through and disappearing. Somebody was shouting far off—I ran back outside.

The shouting was Cleon's—he'd had to wait with held breath while the fight was on, and had seen us and the Pan-Okie men running about, and now could no longer stand it and was bawling for Lena at the top of his lungs. She was picking herself up and yelling at him to shut up—I hailed him and gave him a wave. Suddenly, he spun about and started dancing and grabbing at himself in a way we couldn't fathom—one of the drillers seemed to be following his lead and doing a similar dance step.

What had happened was, in all the confusion, Cleon had failed to notice one of the crew had a small pistol in a flap holster on his belt. Now the three drillers had agreed to use it by nodding at each other when Cleon wasn't looking, but the question was when, since at least at the beginning of the battle Cleon had resisted temptation and kept his eyes on them. But as the battle proceeded, he had begun to steal glances over his shoulder and by now had turned completely away from his prisoners, straining for a sight of his daughter.

This was the moment—with Cleon waving happily to us, the man went for his gun. But because of the way these things go, the latch on the snap stuck, and pull as he did, he couldn't budge it. Cleon sensed this—he spun around.

"Hey, stop that," he said, alarmed.

With a hateful look and some embarrassment, the man continued to tear at his holster flap. Cleon leveled the shotgun at him and pulled the triggers. The hammers fell on empty chamber—he'd of course forgotten to reload after doing Dullnig.

So the dance we saw was Cleon desperately groping through his pocket for shotgun shells and the driller hopping up and down, straining with both hands on the holster flap, in a kind of race. It must have lasted only seconds, but it seemed a long time—Cleon groping, the man tearing. Cleon finally fishing out a shell, the man finally ripping off the flap, Cleon locking the breach, the man drawing the pistol—and both of them firing at once.

Cleon won by a part of a second—at that range, even he couldn't miss and the man was blown away, literally blown away, picked up and thrown in a pile against one of the derrick legs like so much bloody laundry. No longer belligerent, the other two drillers flung themselves off the platform and over the ridge, rolling down the steep slope to the bottom, but Cleon was too stunned by what he'd done to stop them, and we were too far off.

That's not fair, really—we were all stunned by what we saw and the sudden silence that came on us. We staggered toward each other, looking each other over with disbelieving eyes, searching for the sight of the gaping wounds and tattered limbs that should have been there, but for some reason weren't. No, it was clear the blood and wounds were on the other side, the still heaps in the dirt, the pieces of gore, the wreckage of the wagon, the tar-paper shack now burning and crackling merrily from the stove I'd demolished. We, as a matter of strange fact, had captured the hill. Cleon still refused to believe it—he was pulling away his coat and vest, testing his body with ginger hands as if some bullet might have taken away his gut but left no hole by weaving in between the gaps in his clothes, when we heard three sharp blasts of a whistle from down the hill and then the crackle of controlled rifle fire. Hellman was commencing his counterattack.

It was a childish game we played for the next minute, an Easter-egg hunt in the dirt for the grenades that had been scattered this way and that when the wagon had spilled, and settling for much less than all of them, I yelled at the two and herded them toward the far rim, where the rifle fire told me the attack would come. With barely a moment to catch our wind, I spaced us out at ten-foot intervals and made sure each had their grenades piled and handy. The rifle fire was whistling overhead, harmless for the time being—taking a chance to peek over the edge, I could see Hellman had formed his sound men into a line of skirmishers and was moving them smartly up the slope, having them fire from the hip as they climbed to keep our heads down. Hellman himself was anchoring one end of the line—Bliss had the other, and in the breaks in the shooting we could hear them yelling to the line to stay spread and keep up the rate of fire.

Looking things over, I decided not to answer their fire, since that would have sent them to the ground and made their movement one of dash and cover, so we put our guns aside, and as hard as it was for me to resist and as hard as it was for Lena and Cleon to follow my reasoning, we simply lay there panting, waitting for them to be on us. I was in the middle with Cleon on my one hand—I looked over at him, with some surprise noticing what looked like the same sort of blood-lust Lena showed now showing in his face as well.

"Are you all right?" I asked.

"Yeah, yeah," he nodded, amazed that he was. To convince me, he took two grenades, pulled the restraining pins from each, and held them ready in his hands.

The racket of the firing grew deafening as the line neared the top, and you can imagine how tense we were waiting there, but I was hoping that would cut two ways, since the Hellmen had to be more worried by no more answering fire from us than the weak fire of three weapons. It might have been this tension or it might have been Hellman's notion all along, but at that moment, he blew one mighty blast on the whistle, and we could hear him shouting at his men to charge.

The firing stopped—for a bit we heard nothing but the wind whistling, and then from the distance, but growing louder as they came, the sound of boots crunching at a fast pace below us and heavy breathing. I looked over and saw the men, nine of them in a bent but intact line, indeed charging up the remaining fifty yards that separated us. I pulled pins on two grenades myself—from the side of my eye, I saw Lena had done the same. I held back—oh how I held back—until from where I lay pressed flat against the rim hearing those eighteen boots through the dirt, I could just see the tops of two or three black derbies rising into my sight, bobbing like wood chips in a stream, and then I got up to my knees and shouting something for courage hurled both grenades as high and hard as I could, and the other two threw theirs.

The line of men hesitated and slowed as those six grenades arched over the rim and landed, hissing and smoking, at their feet. I saw that much in a glance but I was already priming and throwing another pair, Lena and Cleon likewise, like so many windmills, raining grenades down on the line even though the first volley had yet to go off.

Few of the Hellmen knew what they were—Cleon said he even saw a man prod one with his toe before it went off with a shredding bang and the man disappeared in a gout of smoke, to be seen a moment later rolling head over heels down the slope with his leg flopping from the knee. At that point the hillside blew up—the other two grenades, then the next salvo of three, and more salvos as fast as we unloaded them, with all the blasts blending into one and the smoke and fire flaring and billowing like black soap bubbles, and the air filled with the whiz of steel shreds flying, chewing up flesh unsinged by fire or burst, and bodies soaring this way and that, on their fronts, on their sides, hands to their guts, hands to their faces. Some still came on, five or six, with Hellman prodding from behind, and to stop them from overrunning us, we were forced to blow grenades an arm's length away, cowering flat into the ground under the spread of their blast. One man climbed so close grenades were useless and rifles too awkward–it was arms and legs and feet kicking and Lena yanking his hair, but he was the high-water mark of the assault and once we threw him back, we were hurling grenades again. We didn't let up for an instant, nor budge from our positions, even though the supply of grenades was running down, and lucky for us because at this moment the line started to waver and fall back. One man began the panic, throwing away his rifle and fleeing downslope, and those left still able were quick to follow, some in terror, some with curses, some ignoring the wounded at their feet, and some having the decency to drag them after. Hellman and Bliss were trying to block the route with their arms, then their bodies, but the tide had turned and the line was retreating, ignoring everything but the storm of grenades that still followed them down the slope like so many booming giant footsteps.

In one minute there had been nine of them–in the next there were only two, Hellman and Bliss. Bliss was wounded–Hellman had come through the whole thing unscathed. Bliss looked over at his boss and began to edge away, in a guilty fashion. Hellman watched him silently, turned, and glared up at us, hands in the pockets of his slicker. If I had had a grenade I'd have thrown it, but I was out–Lena had one left and she hurled it right at him with all her force. Hellman saw it coming and who had sent it–she could only loft it halfway down, so it hit short and rolled some before coming to rest maybe ten feet away from him. He eyed it the way he might a dead cat on a sidewalk—Lena held her breath and clenched her fists, waiting for it to go off. It did, but with only a little pop and a puff of smoke—it was a dud, and I was surprised Treadlo hadn't sold us more of them. Hellman smiled darkly, brushed some dust off his slicker with his hand, and strolled back down the slope, presenting us with his back.

It was over. It was all over, without a doubt. I stood up, a little dizzy—Lena and Cleon stood in turn. Suddenly the old man leapt on me with a shout, sticking his head in my face and hugging me, actually trying to lift me off my feet.

"You did it!" he was shouting. "We tore them apart!"

He was right. I roared back with victorious laughter, slapping the top of his head with my hands. "You're a mean son of a bitch yourself, ain't you!"

"Yeah, I am." And when he considered what he'd said, he decided he liked it. "Yeah, I really am, ain't I?" And he turned to Lena and called her name, putting his arm around my shoulder and spinning me around as well so we stood there, linked and grinning, like two heroes at a factory football game.

Lena nodded faintly, turned away from us, and started walking toward the rig. Just like that—no word of thanks, no sign of approval.

That was too much. "You're welcome, lady," I shouted at her, and would have shouted more had not

Cleon shushed me and held me back, saying it was all right.

"What do you mean it's all right?" I yelled, now at him, but he made me shut up and stay put while he followed after Lena. I threw up my hands, disgusted.

She was walking slowly about the rig, watching it move, seeing what changes had been made, studying it all with a loving and kindly look. There was a drilling log in a little box on the headache post—she took it out and flipped through it, scanning the notes. Cleon stood nearby waiting for her to finish, and when she did, she looked up at him with a smile.

"They've hauled in four hundred feet of ten-inch. Four hundred feet of eight-inch. A Smith-Valle bottom pump." She read some more. "A ninety-horse F and T . . ." She flipped to the end. "They're through cap rock and down three hundred and fifty feet." She might have been reading Scripture, so reverent was her voice.

She smiled at Cleon again. He shrugged and smiled back. She put her hand on the king post to feel the vibrations.

It was knowing nothing was settled, that Pan-Oklahoma would never in an eternity let us get away with what we'd done that kept us from any celebration of our triumph, and all we did once Hellman and his survivors in the touring car drove out of sight was bury the stiffs and set about to consolidate our position. I say we, but I mean Cleon and myself—one person had to tend the drilling whenever the rig was running, sitting beside the hole on a little three-legged stool and watching the wire as it rose and fell, letting it down by turning a temper screw, purely by sound and feel, as the bit dug deeper. Since we had to concede that was a skill only she among us had, Lena got to relax while we others passed the morning building a barricade with firing positions around the rim, using sandbags, crates, junk, and whatever else we could find, the most useful being some curved and flanged cast-iron plates Pan-Okie had brought in, scheduled to be bolted together someday into a holding tank. Shoulder-and-leg work like that isn't so bad once you and your partner get the rhythm of it, one man picking while the other shovels, and after a while Cleon and I were working well together, laying the plates and breaking the silence now and then with a snatch of song or a dirty story. We were feeling pretty good—that much she couldn't take away—and we felt like letting it show.

By mid afternoon, we were finished, and for the rest of the day, Cleon and I saw to the necessities, taking an inventory of what Pan-Okie had brought in, counting and storing what ammunition was left, and collecting our provisions. I say ours, but they were really Pan-Okie's as well—we'd brought little with us, partly because we lacked money to buy any and partly because we had relied on the company to have some sort of kitchen for the crew, which was a good assumption, but unfortunately they'd stored their food in the tar-paper shack which I, in my zeal, had caused to burn down that morning. All we were able to salvage from the wreckage was a bag of rice, a case of canned peaches, three bottles of mineral water, and two bottles of cheap whiskey, all of which Lena quickly grabbed for safekeeping and stored in the new iron shack. By some neat rationing, I figured the food could last three weeks, the water maybe half that, but any way we cut it, we'd have to deal with that shortage soon.

As I've said, we were giddy with victory through the morning, but as the afternoon progressed and we found ourselves taking more and more time away from our tasks to glance over our shoulders for any signs of the Hellmen returning, that giddiness was replaced by a growing tenseness, and that tension coupled with simple physical exhaustion left Cleon and me somewhat low by the day's end. Lena, on the other hand, had grown increasingly more good-humored.

This came out when we took our first meal that evening, canned peaches and rice obviously, the three of us sitting together on the rig platform. Lena was casting me and Cleon coy looks and chuckling when we didn't respond.

"What's wrong with you two?" she asked. "You were jumping around like lunatics this morning."

"Hooray," I mumbled.

"I'm pleased for you, Lena," said Cleon quietly. "I really am. And I ain't sorry."

She shook her head. "You don't feel it, do you?"

"Feel what?" wondered Cleon.

"The romance."

We both looked at her closely to see if she was kidding, but she wasn't.

"The romance. You make a hole in the earth and out comes oil. So you sell the oil and sink more wells, and those come in, and pretty soon you have a field." She paused here for a breath, a faraway look on her face. "And you sell stock and you capitalize and you own wells all over the country and you recapitalize and you amalgamate, and now the whole world wants your oil—China and Africa want your oil—and your oil is running lights and machines and trains and ships . . ."

"What about electricity?" I asked.

"You need a waterfall. Oil just needs a flame. Cheaper than coal, more efficient than steam—refine it and you get kerosene, asphalt, naphtha, and gasoline—asphalt for the roads and gas for all the cars on the roads—oil in every home, oil on every wheel . . ."

At this point, she trailed off, seeing the blank and wondering expressions we gave her. Obviously she was wasting her pearls on us swine.

She stood. "I pity you," she said. "I'm turning in. You figure out your own guard shifts." She started to walk away, then turned back. "The iron shack's mine. Sleep where you want." And on that note of hospitality, she was gone.

Cleon and I ate in silence for a while. Finally he looked up, wiping his chin.

"What do you suppose she meant by the romance of oil?"

I thought it over—then I pointed at the shaft with the stiff cable riding up and down inside it. My meaning was that what Lena saw as romance, I saw as merely somebody fucking and somebody else getting fucked, as indicated by stroke of the cable and the receptivity of the hole.

Cleon considered for a while. "I think it meant she's pleased."

I shook my head. As hard as I tried, I couldn't see how he came to that conclusion.

We two slept that evening but Lena didn't, staying up with her rig through the night and making hole. The early morning found us back at work, lubricating and polishing and putting things in order, preferring to keep mindlessly busy rather than wonder where the Hellmen were or how many they would be. And past noon, just at the point we were allowing ourselves to wonder if by some stroke they weren't coming back at all, Lena, from her vantage point on the platform, let out a yell and pointed off. We knew what that meant—without fuss and with a certain resignation, we shut down the rig and gathered our weapons and what grenades remained and took our positions behind the barricade.

The first sight we well expected, being the touring car, once more emerging from the same rise behind which it had disappeared the previous day. Following it by a few yards came a stake truck with a tarp over its bed so its load was hidden, but that there was a crowd of armed men beneath wasn't that hard to presume. But what jolted us and froze our hearts was the next truck and the truck that followed it and all those others, ten in all, truck after truck after truck coming into sight in turn and trailing Hellman toward us in a long, slow convoy.

Lena had been nodding with narrow eyes at the first truck or so, but as each new one emerged, that look had blanched somewhat and her eyes had widened a percentage, so by the time all ten were below us at the base spreading out to unload, I could hear her whispering, "Oh, Jesus," to herself, over and over. And well put, because when the tailgates fell, perhaps sixty men with rifles spilled out, milling about in some confusion, while Hellman bawled orders from the running board of his car and the Hellmen herded them into rough formations. I could recognize some by their dress and stance even at this distance—at least half were my former buddies from the hobo camp, which meant Hellman was paying.

So there we were, well doomed. It was sad. It had been nice to have our triumph and we had to be grateful for whatever time given us to savor it, but that time was over. It was too much to watch all that preparation, so I pulled back behind my iron slab, elbows on my knees, and simply waited for what would follow. Lena and Cleon slumped on either side of me, equally miserable.

"I never thought they'd go that far," Cleon said softly. Lena groaned—Cleon himself realized how dumb what he just said had been, because he sighed and shut up again, like us, listening to the far-off sounds of orders shouted and truck transmissions grinding. Squirming on his ass, he couldn't take simply waiting either, so he turned to peer down once more. His gasp startled us all.

"Tents! Look at them all—tents!"

And looking for ourselves, we saw he was absolutely right. The groups had been told off not into assault parties but into work crews—out of one of the vans had fallen a number of white bundles, which when rolled out proved to be pyramid tents, and the crews were erecting them along the lines of a very proper bivouac.

We might have stayed there for hours, mouths hung open, in astonishment, had we not been brought to by the toot of a car horn, and when we stood, seen the sight of the touring car struggling up the road toward us with a white flag tied prominently to a pole. Too confused to do anything but react, we hurried over behind the iron shack to cover its approach.

But like somebody motoring to a Sunday trout stream, the car drove up nice as you please and stopped in the open. Bliss as usual was driving—he got out and opened the rear door for Hellman, who stretched a bit as he stood and then motioned a third man to exit. This turned out to be a young gentleman with brilliantined hair and a smart suit with a celluloid collar, the sneer of a bully but the prissy air of one who still kisses his momma good-night, and there they stood, no arms showing, obviously come to parlay and waiting for an audience.

That we were less than eager to give one might have been just as obvious by the way we found ourselves shoving pistols in our belts and hanging grenades on our shirt flaps, in general trying to appear as bloodthirsty as three Huks come from an opium den. And of all of us, the most bold was the least eager, since as we stepped forth at last to meet them, with both Cleon and I allowing the other the honor of being first, she hung back a bit, and when I turned to her, she motioned me on, saying, "You see what he wants" and followed a few paces behind. Perhaps Hellman being once more so close had caused her old bruises to tingle somewhat.

Hellman and the young man traded looks as we hove into sight.

"I never did get your name," Hellman said to me, friendly enough.

"Mason."

"Of course—Mr. Mason. You've met Bliss. This is Mr. Henry H. Wilcox, from our Tulsa office." He nodded at the young man.

"Harrison Wilcox's kid," muttered Lena, speaking the name of Mr. Pan-Oklahoma himself.

"He is indeed," smiled Hellman, pointing her out to young Wilcox. "Miss Doyle over there. And you must be her father, Mr. Holder."

Cleon nodded, begrudging that. With the introductions over, Hellman took Wilcox by the arm and began to escort him toward the derrick without a by-your-leave, even though their course took them directly into Cleon, who shuffled backward at a loss, raising his shotgun to block them.

Hellman halted, all polite. "I'm sorry. Of course—may we?"

Lena gave Cleon a little nod, at which point he

backed away and the three of them breezed past. We looked at each other and then followed, seeing as if we didn't on our own, we weren't about to be invited.

While Bliss stood away, Hellman was taking Wilcox on a guided tour of the equipment. The young man was studying the tower and the machinery and making clucking noises. "Cable tools?" he kept saying over and over, in disbelief.

"You were using them," I replied.

Hellman turned to me with a kindly look. "There isn't any water on the tract. A rotary takes water, as you know."

He said that sarcastically, as if I didn't, but I did, at least somewhat. Rotary rigs were just coming into fashion then—the difference between them and the older cable rigs was that the cable rigs operated by a percussion principle, like putting a drill bit in a brace and simply dropping the affair over and over onto the same spot on a piece of wood; it would make a hole sooner or later, but it was a lot faster to lay the bit against the wood and turn it, the principle of the rotary. The only remaining advantage of cable tools was that you could pull the tool string from the hole and scoop out your diggings, while a rotary remained in the hole at all times, being lengthened by adding on pipe to the part that stuck out above the shaft, and depended on a constant flow of water down the hole to flush it clean. You sunk pipe down a cable-tool hole as well, but only to shore up the sides when you ran into water or layers of heaving sand that would cave in otherwise.

But before I could set Hellman right, Wilcox had

gone onto his next point, being the casing just mentioned, since he had looked over the waiting stacks on the hill and had decided they were insufficient.

"She counted it—there's six hundred feet," Cleon piped up, despite his nervousness.

Hellman turned his smile on him. "You tell her as a matter of record, there hasn't been a well in twenty miles brought in under two thousand."

Now this was news to both Cleon and me, and made us turn to Lena, whose only reply was to avoid our eyes. It would have been somewhat fairer had she told us about those two-thousand-foot holes at the outset, I remember thinking, but at that moment Hellman jolted me with his shoulder as he pushed past, arm in arm with Wilcox again, now leading him over to the slush-pit. Hellman kneeled down at the edge of that muddy pool, took off a glove, and dipped a finger in. He tasted it and shook his head.

"Salt and sulphur."

With another sneer for us all, he stood and began to put on his glove again.

"You got no business here, Hellman," Lena burst out finally. "You're just wacking off for the boy!"

As all of us did the first few times with Lena, Wilcox blushed and sputtered. Hellman was unmoved.

"Now you know what Miss Doyle is most famous for," he said, taking Wilcox once more by the arm and leading him back toward the car, the grand tour apparently over.

In all of this, our puzzlement hadn't lessened, but the

truth of what this was all about suddenly came through to Lena.

"You're cutting us off–is that it?" she called out to Hellman's back.

He slowly turned around. "I assumed you'd realize that. Of course–those men down there are to keep you on this hill, not put you off. We're putting you under a state of siege."

"You remember," Wilcox added gaily. "From your history books. Where everybody in the castle dies."

Cleon was flabbergasted. "He can't do it," he croaked. "We can use the road . . ."

"No you can't," Hellman cut in, sharply. "It's a Pan-Oklahoma road, not a public one. You actually can't go anywhere–all you can do is sit on your hill and fiddle with your broken-down rig with no tools, no water, no casing . . ."

"That's enough!" Lena yelled, loud enough to make us all start. "Fine–you do what you have to do, Captain."

Cleon wasn't so anxious to stop the negotiations, but when he began to speak again, Lena yelled, "I said enough!" just as loud once more, with the impression she'd yell those words over and over at him until he shut up.

Hellman looked satisfied with the mood he'd created. "We will do what we have to, Miss Doyle," he said. "We have already." With that he headed for his car again–without turning, he added, "Oh, when you decide you've had enough you might raise a flag similar to that one," and he pointed at the white flag on his car.

The meeting might have ended there, with the three of us armed to teeth watching in a stunned way as the other three, with not a dull pocketknife between them, drove off totally triumphant. Instead, Hellman paused at the car and motioned to me with a finger. I looked at Lena, considered—then followed. He pulled me off to one side as if to tell me some secret, but not so far that we were out of her sight, surely his intention, as was the worried look that came over her face.

"I should have paid you when you offered me the chance," he began, in a chummy way.

I almost agreed with him, so right was he as I saw it, but something stopped me from replying at all.

"Well, look what happened." He mused for a bit. "You know, if you came along with me now, I bet I could turn up that money someplace."

Keep in mind this was what I had wanted from the first, all I had ever wanted, and even after going in with Lena, I knew I still wanted it somewhat. But too many things had come between me and my ambitions in the last few days, so I still couldn't answer directly, and when I finally said, "I honestly don't know," I wasn't being coy.

He figured I was. "I know—you'd like to stick around and see me squirm a little. That's your mistake—you're taking this personally. I won the last round. You win this one. I admit it. You're still a businessman, aren't you?"

He might have had me right there. I can still feel the way my body swayed in his direction, but at that point, like so many clever persons, he began to undo himself.

"On the other hand, being your partner, she might be providing you with something no man can give." And he tilted his head at Lena.

That irritated me a little. If I was being provided by Lena, it was none of his affair, but of course it was obvious to all I wasn't, and if that was so obvious, why'd he have the bad taste to ask?

"That would be the worst motive of all for a businessman like yourself," he went on. "I'm speaking of course of a bit of snatch."

Normally that shouldn't have offended me. I was a businessman, had used the term myself many times. And Lena was in fact a bit of snatch, and for the world's purposes little else. Why then did I blush and fume and look away from Hellman and down at my feet, seeing Bull sniffing good-naturedly among them?

"Just business reasons, you mean," I said.

"Make the world go around."

At this point I realized I'd forgotten who Hellman was and what he meant to me. I put the muzzle of my carbine up under his chin and gave it a little shove, to pin him there while I thought. I wanted to do something to him—I wanted to say something clever or hit him good, or both, but I couldn't think of the right combination, so to keep things current I thumbed back the carbine's hammer. Hellman didn't blink—his eyes bored into me.

My idea finally arrived—with my free hand I began to open my fly. Hellman noted that—head erect, he strained to look down past his nose at what I was up to, but I kept his chin high with the muzzle as I reached in my skivvies and pulled out my member, which, not to give the impression I can do these things on command, had been sending me messages of urgency ever since I'd first spotted the sixty men come to get us. Now finding a chance for relief, it took it, not caring at what it was pointing, which happened to be the middle of Hellman's slicker. I don't remember the relieving was more or less pleasurable than ever before or since—it was merely the wheels of forces turning, and it seemed to be more something of great forces to be pissing all over Hellman than any private notion of mine.

For the first time since I'd known the man, he turned pale. "You're making a gigantic mistake," he whispered, as he felt the piss pooling about his boots.

"Oh, c'mon—businessmen do this to each other all the time," I answered, flush with the moment. Out of the corner of my eye, I saw Bull cocking his leg and peeing on a rock—I suppose he'd been watching and had been inspired.

Finished, I did what men do, which is wring the thing of its last drops, and giving Hellman a smile similar to his own, turned on my heel and walked off, buttoning up my fly as I went. Behind me I could hear him yanking off the fouled coat with a ripping of seams, but I paid him no mind nor Lena who, amazed at my action, whispered hoarsely as I passed.

"Now you've done it. You're stuck here."

"I know, I know . . ." I replied.

"I don't need any favors," she went on, but I hissed her quiet and strolled on to the shack where I took cover in the cool shade of the overhang, watching nonchalantly what would follow.

Hellman was coming to a boil—his control going and his style demolished. Bliss and Wilcox were trying to force him into the car, but he was resisting, and finally threw them off, spun about and bellowed at us in a raging, screeching voice:

"All right—you've got your hill! I hope you learn to love it! I hope you learn to eat it and drink it because if you don't, I'm going to make sure you two-bit little shitboxes die one hell of a miserable death up here!" And he actually shook his fist at me.

With a great heave, the other two pushed him inside. Bliss hurried into the front seat, started up, and very quickly the touring car with its flag whipping and Hellman livid behind the isinglass had turned in its tracks and trundled down the dome road and out of sight.

Lena turned to me. "Now you've done it," she repeated.

Of course I had, but I didn't feel it, not just then. I knew what a siege meant, thanks to Sir Walter Scott—I'd read of knights scaling walls and the boiling oil poured and the slow starvation—but for some reason, the notion of being trapped on that hill didn't affect me that much. Maybe I was just tired after all that effort or maybe it was just the idea I no longer had any choice, that like Lena had said, I was stuck there for good, that gave me a certain sort of peace. After a life of having all the choices in the world and making them all wrong, the notion of having no alternatives came as a sort of holiday. It was a strange feeling.

At any rate, Lena's spirits began to revive on their own, what with Hellman physically gone. She paced, thinking—then she turned to us.

"He'd take us if he thought he could. What's stopping him?"

We just waited for her answer.

"Pan-Okie's stopping him, that's what. This thing's gotten out of hand, or else why is Wilcox's kid here?" She paced some more, apparently liking what she'd said. "Sure—of course. We can eat jackrabbits. We can catch rain water. Figure it out—if he was going to take us, he would have just done it. It's all bluff."

I noticed Cleon was eyeing the same thing I was, namely Hellman's crumpled slicker left there in the dirt, so he was probably having doubts similar to mine.

But Lena seemed in fine fettle—she crossed to the gas engine, checked the spark, cranked it, and the engine sputtered to life in an accommodating way. Getting it up to speed, she engaged the drive belt, and with a creak the walking beam began its rise and fall once more, and the rig was back in operation. As if that were her final statement on the matter, she returned to her stool and sat with a smile of satisfaction.

While I stood in thought, Cleon came over and

nudged me, pointing. What with the sound of the drill striking rock far below, thousands of jackrabbits had popped out of the holes they'd occupied while the rig had been shut down and were scampering terrified in a wave down the slope, racing for the open. I considered pointing that out to Lena, but I didn't.

14

The whole purpose of an oil rig is to make a foot-wide hole in the ground down through various layers of rock and dirt to a point where, for a reason as far as I have heard nobody's figured out, there may be a pool of oil waiting to bubble up to the surface, given the right circumstances such as not too much sand and shit mixed in and a little natural gas to give it a shove. Being anything more complicated than that has always been lost on me—it's all machinery to sink a drill, the star of the show, along with its tool string, the auger stem, jars, and rope socket, the jars being just a hunk of metal that slides up and down on a shaft to give the drill a kick as it bites. Then there's a hundred feet or so of manila rope tied on called a cracker, also used for its snapping action, and finally the stiff six-wind steel cable itself that runs up the hole and connects to the walking beam at the temper screw. The walking beam is a great log of wood pivoted in the middle on a Sampson post so it swings up and down like a teeter-totter—as it moves, so naturally does the tool string far down the bore, and the beam itself gets its motion from a pitman arm, which is fixed in eccentric to a large flywheel called a band wheel, thus converting circular motion to up-and-down, and that in turn is spun by a twelve-inch canvas belt running between it and the pulley of the engine unit further back. The engine also drives two or three drums by means of belts and clutches—the bull wheel, which handles the cable, lowering it or drawing it out either to clear the hole for the bailer or to sharpen the bit, the calf wheel, which lowers casing when it's needed, and the sand wheel, which lowers the bailer. The tower itself, which looks like what the rig is all about, is actually the least important, being useful only when spudding in the hole, meaning the first thirty feet or so when there's not enough room to swing the regular tool string from the walking beam, and you hang a special bit and work it through the cathead or crown-block pulley at the derrick peak on a jerkline, and later on, if you have to drop casing. Since the casing pipe came in twenty-foot lengths and it was easier to set two lengths at a time, that called for a derrick at least forty feet high to hoist them clear, and most derricks were taller, around eighty.

Now this may seem like very little in the way of a description of an oil rig, but in fact it's all a man of common sense needs to know, and I wish somebody could have taught it to me as briefly and with as much care to explain what all the strange words like sampson post and spudding meant. Inventing a lingo to me is the product of men at a dull task trying to make it sound complicated, usually to impress somebody, and it's been years since I amused myself with the knowledge I was speaking of things only one out of ten men around me could understand. I used to go on—I would say things like, "There was a cat's ass in the line so bad I had to take a preacher's prick to it," and think myself quite a rake, but then I was in a grocery store one day and heard the term preacher's prick applied by the grocer to that stick thing with jaws he use to fish cans off the high shelves, and I've been simply saying kinks in the cable and wrenches ever since.

But then I've found that there are few things in the world that require more than five minutes to describe, and Lena fell well within that space that afternoon as she gave me my first lessons in drilling. It was necessity, not particularly good will, that brought her to it, since she had two men to choose from for help, and while she truly didn't want one to touch her rig, she didn't want the other to come within twenty feet of it. Cleon got the job of permanent guard—while Pan-Okie claimed they were going to starve us out, there was no point in believing them. Being in Lena's interest to make hole as fast as we could, that meant we had to drill around the clock, so we worked out an optimistic schedule of hours on and hours off, one that would normally burn out a crew in a week.

And while we settled down to our routine that day and the next—Lena on the cable, logging the progress, me doing the odd jobs and the messy ones, Cleon marching the perimeter with his shotgun in the hot sun—so did the Pan-Okie camp. They'd laid out guards of their own, but that only depleted them by a third or so, which meant there were at least forty men still in camp, as far as we could observe, doing nothing at all except standing in line for everything—meals, water, and latrines. Faint sounds of laughter or singing would come up to us now and then, the kind you would hear from a distant panic, and the comparison isn't that bad since those men were on the payroll for their presence more than their labor, and had I been employed under such circumstances, I would have sung myself.

It took us only about a week of hard labor for the strain to begin to show. I wasn't shaving, since the only water to be had outside of the dwindling bottles was the sulphurous stuff you could get out of the slushpit by squeezing some of the mud through a rag, and that seemed more trouble than it was worth. The same with bathing—I'd work up a fine smelly sweat during the hot day, transfer part of it to my bedding when I slept that night, but have enough left over to make my arms stick to my flanks when I tried to raise them the next morning. The tin hats we wore for safety purposes, since parts were always falling off those old rigs, only served to make a little oven to cook your hair and brains and leave the one matted and the other addled. It was no pleasure to experience and, since the same was happening to my partners, no pleasure to witness, and to keep our temper, we soon learned to concentrate on our tasks and ignore the shade and comfort of those camped below us.

Cleon had started out trying to keep our spirits high, what with retelling the story of our victory, funny songs and jokes he'd heard, and giving fancy French names to the peaches and rice as he spooned them out at mealtimes, but in a few days he tired of that, what with our not encouraging him, and fell into a moody silence that matched ours. Still, around the end of that first week, as he was making his rounds, he broke his silence with a shout that brought me running and even caused Lena to take the band wheel out of gear and follow me over to the rim.

He was pointing south at a plume of dust traveling slowly across the expanse. It was a single car, muddy and beat up, with all sorts of camping gear lashed to its sides, and as we walked around with it, it made a circuit of the dome and pulled up on the county road away from the Hellman camp. There were two men in the car—one got out and stretched. He must have been somebody, since we could see Hellman himself walking out from the camp along with Bliss and Wilcox to meet him halfway. He was old, as we could tell from his gait, and he shook hands with Hellman and then Wilcox in a familiar way.

Beside me, Lena was shading her eyes and straining to see. Then she grunted.

"You know them?" I asked.

"Deke Watson. That's his partner C. R. Miller in the car. They scout for Tri-State."

"So?"

"So that's just fine."

It seemed to be some kind of argument—Hellman shook his head and then turned his back and stomped off. While Watson waited, Wilcox ran after Hellman and took him by the shoulder, spoke for a while, and finally coaxed him back to the group, against what appeared to be his will.

"They've heard what happened and they've come to watch," Lena said, looking smug. "They know Pan-Okie is stuck—they've come to camp out and see what happens."

Sure enough, after more parley, the two finally shook hands, and while Hellman and his party returned to camp, Watson started back for his car waving to his buddy who immediately began to dump off their camping gear in a heap.

"Hellman don't dare refuse him," Lena went on. "It's a courtesy among companies. They won't try to get up to me since its through Pan-Okie land, but when I bring it in, they'll be up here bidding their ass off." With a snort, she left us and headed back for the rig.

Cleon and I exchanged glances. "You think she's right?" he wondered.

Lena could probably read our minds from our faces, for she called back to us: "And they'll be more of them. You watch—when it comes in, Hellman will have to climb over everybody else to be the first with a purchase contract."

Out by their car, Watson and Miller were wrestling with an old patched tent and staking it down, that much was sure.

But nobody else came after and the peaches soon ran out and the hole got deeper by about thirty feet every day. I didn't know at the time that we were damn lucky even to do that well without some major setback, but everything held, and outside of having to sharpen the bit every night, which was its own kind of bitch, seeing as you had to get it red hot on a wood fire, difficult enough, and then pound it with sledges on an anvil to get its edge back and then douse it in the slushpit fast enough so the temper wasn't lost, which meant lots of fancy handling and some mistakes, one of which I still bear in the form of a scar that looks like a piece of pink silk sewn to my hip, the hole went deeper through blue shale and light shale, hard sand and soft, lime and slate, all properly recorded by Lena in the log she kept.

Our friendships, never that solid to begin with, suffered with the weeks of ordeal and I suppose it was only the fact we were too weary to start them that kept us from fistfights. We went back to grunt language and forbore that if a finger or a pointed shoulder would do the job. Perhaps our only consolation was that those below us were beginning to feel the pinch as well—the holiday spirit was fading, what from the fact that some of the hidden clauses in the Hellman contract had come out, being bad food, rationed water, and, more than anything, boredom and a burning sun to be bored in. Some tents in the camp had shade flies, but only those of the Hellmen themselves, who would lounge there all day in wicker chairs reading newspapers and playing cards, which did nothing to increase the solidarity between the bums and them. But then the bums being bums, they took to going around half naked, some with nothing but a loin cloth, while the Hellmen, being gentlemen and professionals and feeling the need to uphold their dignity, kept their shirt sleeves buttoned and a neat tie around their wilting collars, which couldn't have brought them much comfort either.

Then one night we discovered oil, or at least the showings of it. I'd noticed a scum forming on top of the mud in the slushpit and I mentioned it to Lena. She took a lantern off its hook and we both bent down to study it—the scum was a film, obviously separating out from the diggings and, being lighter, floating to the surface. In the light it spread in swirls, all colored like a rainbow. Lena took a stick and stirred it—the swirls broke but flowed back together when the stirring stopped. As a final test, Lena stuck her finger in the film and tasted a drop of it.

"That's it," she said.

"How about that." I was impressed.

She merely stood and walked over to the log. "You

think I'd really go through all this if I didn't know there was oil here?"

"You couldn't have known."

"I knew," she said.

"You never knew."

She looked at me—and then looked away. "It's here. It's just further down." She sat back on her perch by the cable.

So that was it—we'd just struck oil. All it made me feel was weary. I sat on the platform near her, and just how tired I was after weeks of wrestling with steel bits and stiff iron cable and fifty-gallon gas drums came over me. While I was considering that, Cleon loomed into the yellow glow from the kerosene lanterns, just wordlessly passing on his patrol. And it occurred to me that as tired as I was, I'd gotten some few hours of sleep the previous night, and he hadn't.

"That's his third shift," I said.

She looked over at Cleon but only nodded.

"Why don't I relieve him?"

"It's not your turn."

"I ain't as tired as he is."

"Let him stay."

I nodded—all right, if that's what she wanted. She could work that old man until his knees were his feet if she wanted—it was her choice, though it seemed less than fair to do it.

Maybe Lena noted something of disapproval in my look. "If he wants to take extra shifts, that's up to him."

"Sure." I wasn't looking for any argument.

But I could see something spreading in her face, even in that dim yellow light, something like shame the way her eyes followed Cleon out of the glow and back into the dark again.

"I got the answer for you," I said.

"Answer for what?"

"Your thing with your pa."

She scowled, meaning she wasn't interested, but I felt like going on.

"You ought to both strip down to your undies and lock yourselves in the iron shack. Each of you takes a sack filled with horseshit and starts beating up the other one until you kill each other."

"That's not funny," she mumbled.

I shrugged—I thought it was a little bit funny.

"Anyway, it's none of your business."

"Yeah," I said, and then paused. "He ain't so bad though."

"Try hating him for twenty-five years." She thought some more. "Try hating him in two centuries."

But when she said those words, she seemed uncomfortable with them, as if she herself were a little shocked by their sound. Maybe saying it out loud was different than merely thinking it.

At that point Cleon came back into sight and waved at us in greeting as he usually did. He must have been surprised to see both of us staring at him, because his smile turned sort of wavering and self-conscious as he passed through our view.

15

The days dragged past, which is not to say nothing happened, but means nothing much happened that strikes the memory. True, we had our problems—a hard shale that slowed us down greatly, flesh that began to blister and peel in the sun—and of course the exhaustion grew out of hand, since we all knew, Hellman and us, that three people simply cannot run a rig around the clock no matter how they try. There were times I'd fall asleep in the act of hauling on a line, Cleon would lean up against a shack wall for a breather and we'd find him there hours later, and Lena actually fell off her stool in a dead faint once, so now and then we'd have to shut down completely, matching coins to see who stayed awake on guard while the other two collapsed. Still and all, the hole progressed and by the end of six weeks we were down 850 feet, with no real oil yet, but, according to Lena, plenty of favorable showings.

Then one night there was no rice anymore. Nobody said anything, but the next day Cleon served up a soup of greens, being a little water in a cup with some bristly things swimming in it, which turned out to be weeds he'd picked off the hilltop. Then the water itself ran out—by now Cleon had harvested the dome top clean and was forced to go looking beyond the barricade. I was working the bailer one morning when I heard a bullet ricochet and threw myself down, figuring the attack was beginning. But none followed, and when I looked over, I saw Cleon squirming backward behind one of the iron plates—he had a handful of prairie grass and had been stretching out to get more when somebody down at the wire had shot at him out of pure tedium, and come close enough to fill his eyes with dirt. He picked himself up and stumbled over to the platform, all the time trying to flood his eyes and get the grit out, mashed the grass in a tin can, and emptied into it all that was left in the last water bottle.

Lena and I both had the same idea, but she got there first, grabbed the bottle, and winding up threw it over the barricade. We heard it smash on the slope—then sat down to our breakfast, her and I taking a handful of the grass and chewing it slowly.

After a while I noticed Cleon hadn't touched his third of the weeds. I offered the pot to him.

He shook his head. "My stomach can't handle that stuff," he said and motioned to us to finish it off.

There were clouds in the next few days, rolling gray ones plump with rain, but they passed overhead as we watched without giving up a drop. It might have been all that exhaustion just building up, or it might have been our starving stomachs, but all the sitting on the bad temper we'd managed so far started breaking down around then. We began to gripe and bitch at each other when we collided, and roused each other roughly from our sleep when our shifts were over. Though we slept we never were rested, and eating wasn't worth the effort because the weeds gave you no particular energy and the saliva you used to get them down was that much less water to be had. I stopped shitting altogether and pissing was as painful as having all your teeth pulled at once. The only true food left on that entire dome was each other, and while I don't claim we ever got close to that, I do remember having moments when I would regard Cleon and Lena in a different way than usual, namely as so much meat on the hoof, and once you have thoughts like that you're far, far down the road.

And then we found water but the wrong kind of water, a layer of it 930 feet down that came gushing up the hole as sour and poisonous as could be, that stopped our drilling and threatened to cave in the bore if we didn't seal it off, which meant we now had to drop casing. This called for all kinds of extra effort, drawing out the tool string, hanging a traveling block from the top of the derrick, and disconnecting the walking beam from the pitman and swinging it upright to clear it out of the way. Then there was the matter of muscling the lengths of twelve-inch off their stacks and over to the derrick, coupling two lengths together with a threaded collar that you worked with pipe wrenches called tongs, and with the line off the band wheel, through the crown block at the peak, hoisting the coupled length up inside the derrick, swinging it over the hole, and lowering it down, letting it hang there with maybe a foot of it sticking out until you could couple the next length on, and all this with that useless salt water spraying all over you to sting your peeled flesh and make you lose footing.

Lena's poor-boy equipment now began to pay her back for her economy, seeing as the casing was all well used and the threads were all rusted on the collars and pipes, which meant they were that much harder to screw together, us having to scrape off the male and female threads with wire brushes and when that failed, breaking through the rust simply by forcing the lengths together and hoping the turning threads would clean themselves. The right way to do it is to wrap chain around the pipe and let the engine do the rotating, but we were without enough chain to reach and when we tried rope and cable, it wouldn't bite on the greasy pipe, so the job was left up to our backs and arms.

Each joint took time and effort, but each had sooner or later cracked and we were advancing slowly. Then later in the afternoon, we came to one length that wouldn't budge at all, no matter how we kicked and cursed it. I was ready to quit, and I don't mean simply that hopeless task but the whole job—I was at that particular point willing to let those twenty turns of rusty thread provide my end to the oil business, but Lena only prodded me on, took a new bite with her tongs, and since she was scarlet from the exertion and was stretched out straining, practically parallel with the platform floor, looking ready to burst like a balloon filling, I wearily joined in and we shoved together. But her wrench wasn't well set, and as we heaved with all our might its teeth lost grip and she went flying forward, slipping on the wet floor, arcing headlong five feet through the air, and crumpling into a tangle of arms and legs against the sampson post.

She looked dead—Cleon came running and I hastened to where she lay. I reached down to help her—eyes shut, she still shoved my hands away and pulled herself up to a sitting position. She took a deep breath, shook her head clear, and then in a slow way, since she wasn't sure which parts of her were still working, got to her feet while Cleon and I stood waiting to catch her if she keeled.

But she didn't—she blew up instead, yanked up that set of tongs, which was maybe fifteen pounds of tool, and swinging it around like a club, attacked the rig, screaming like a banshee, gouging timbers, clanging casing, yelling "Goddamn lousy fucking piece of shit rig" at the top of her lungs. She smashed the log box, cracked a cast-iron brace, and then went for the casing cable, which only coiled around her arms and made her even more furious. She ripped free—Cleon, who like me had been astounded by this show, now ran after to hold her down, but as he came on she saw him, wound up, and swung for his head with a shriek. Terrified he ducked, lost footing himself, and fell at her feet—she wound up again, throwing those tongs up high, preparing to split him in two like a log, but I managed to get his hand and pull him off the platform and into the dirt just as those tongs came down with a crunch, digging two inches deep into the pine flooring.

She stopped suddenly. We just looked up at her from where we were sprawled. We were in her power at that moment and she was in ours, meaning we wouldn't have the strength to stop her from murdering us both, but then that wasn't what she wanted at all, in fact the last thing she wanted, but what she did want from us, meaning sympathy or comfort or the last ounce from our arms, she was still too stupid and stubborn to ask for. So we remained alive, and she just sat down limp with her feet hanging over the platform edge and started to sob.

That evening before it got dark, a family of carrion crows took up residence on the gin pole of the derrick far over our heads. It was around then I realized things were getting out of hand.

Starvation will do things to a man—I knew a fellow in South Dakota who took a trip during the winter and got lost, and then his horse went lame, so he shot the horse and gutted it and crawled inside the carcass and sat there through a week of blizzard, eating what he'd removed, and when the storm was over he wrapped his legs with hide and struggled through fifty miles of mountains until he found shelter. He received some notice in the papers for his feat and was called a hero, but those who knew him and something of what he'd been through figured he'd gotten inside his horse because he was cold and walked to safety because he was hungry. Most of what the world calls heroism I call an empty stomach, and given our situation, it shouldn't come as much surprise that the next night, while Lena was nodding at the rig and Cleon was stumbling around the rim, I stuck a pistol in my waistband, slung our canteens over my shoulders, and slipped past the barricade and down the dark slope, heading for the Hellman camp below. My reasoning was simple—that's where the food was.

I don't want anyone to think I did this fearlessly, with head held high. That fellow from South Dakota told me he was in fear of his life every minute of the ordeal, but he found the strength to go on because he was just as afraid to either die alone on a mountain trail or suffer the shame of being found dead inside a horse by someone he might have known. I suppose I felt somewhat similar—scared as I was, if I had to go, I wanted to be found with a quiet stomach and full kidneys, and since everything pointed to our end anyway, it seemed no particular gamble.

Things had gotten kind of lax in the Hellman camp

what with the passage of time—I managed to get off the dome and under the wire without seeing a soul, and I made a nice wide loop through the brush and the darkness on my hands and knees to come in on the camp from its far side. I stopped short when I spotted the gray outlines of the first row of tents—I could hear distant voices and, not that happy with the prospect of using it, I drew my pistol and crept slowly forward to take my bearings.

A number of men were still up despite the hour, sitting and shooting the shit around their fires. In the middle of the camp was the chow truck, lit by its own cooking fire—scouting things over, I made out Bloom at the Hellman tent smoking a pipe and then Rucker strolling down an aisle with a white dressing around his head giving a raise to his derby, a wound I had put there, it occurred to me. Near at hand was a listerbag full of water, one of a number hung on a tripod of poles scattered around the camp, and I decided I'd try for that first. But the time for creeping and crawling was over, since the waterbag sat well within the camp perimeter, surrounded by tents and the snoring men inside them, so I finally stood erect, shoved the gun out of sight, smoothed down my pants and coat, and taking out the canteens I'd hidden, walked boldly into the bounds of the camp itself as if I properly belonged there.

True, it was dark and one man looks much like the next in such conditions but still, passing a month or two with sixty men, you'd learn to recognize their various sounds and smells, so as I strolled on, cool on the outside, my guts were tumbling, fearing for one that all eyes were on me and for two that all knew me for a stranger, but thinking that thought, I found myself closing on the listerbag without an alarm yet sounded. I looked to neither side, reached the bag, and bending over shoved the spigot into my mouth and turned it full on, letting my parched body fill, having lost all control at this last moment, with the water spilling down my face and arms and my gulps sounding loud as cannon fire in my ears. Choking a little, feeling my wrinkled skin take up the water like a blotter, I listened, but heard only normal chatter and distant crickets.

But as I began to fill the canteens, there was a sudden rustle of canvas behind me that made me jump. Looking, I saw a man in his long johns step from behind a nearby tent flap and stagger toward me. My hand went for the pistol butt, but luckily I didn't pull it, because instead of challenging me, the man simply got in line behind, shivering and scratching his scalp, waiting for me to finish. When he caught my glance, he nodded me a sleepy good-evening and yawned.

The canteens full, I stepped aside to screw on the lids. As the man came forward to drink, the thought suddenly struck me like a pool ball dropping into a pocket—I was in no danger. I knew it as well as I'd ever known anything—it just came to me at that moment that I did belong there. Being worn-out and rundown, the bums accepted me as one of them—my moves and all may have been unfamiliar, but not so much to scare anybody, and while this realization didn't do anything for my self-esteem, it was my total being that concerned me, and I was willing to trade that minor insult for my skin. My insides calmed—I might have even turned a little cocky. I do know I stepped toward the chow truck upright and loose, for some reason convinced I was going to pull it off, convinced some grace floated around me and was going to keep me safe until I was finished.

And wrapped in that grace, I moved through the enemy. Nothing fazed me, not even turning the corner and coming on Hellman himself, having his boots shined by one of the bums. Bull at his side perked his ears and whined a bit, but I simply doubled back out of sight and found a different route, closing on the chow truck, which I couldn't see what with the tents blocking my sight, but could locate just by the sweet odors that spread from it.

I must admit some of my flame went out when I came on the chow truck itself. This was no longer a matter of skulking in shadows—the truck was well in the open, well lit, manned by two brawny cooks serving food to a line of maybe six or seven men. The cooks I figured I might bluff—it was the line of bums that worried me, the notion of rubbing shoulders with them in the light and my face being recognized, so I hid in the dark for a while hoping the line would thin long enough to get me in and out, but it seemed for every man that walked off with a heaping tin tray, another got in at the head of the line with an empty one. The longer I stalled, the harder those odors worked on me—eventually they all pulled together and I found myself in the light, boldly walking up to the line, picking up a tray, and shuffling along with the others.

"How much is that by the month?" one fellow was saying. By chance, I had joined a discussion on finances.

"I don't know—you figure it," said another.

"Seven-fifty is what it is," said a third. "Fifteen bucks for two months."

They were talking about their pay. While they went on, I filled the pockets of my coat with rolls from a stack at hand. Two more men got in line behind me so I was well wedged in, stuck there for better or worse.

"Can't do much with that," said the second man.

Now somebody spoke from behind me. "You could buy a suit."

"Maybe they'll hold out three months," said the first.

"No chance," answered the second.

"If they do, it's twenty-two fifty," said the third.

At this point I'd reached a neatly stacked pile of sandwiches. The top one had gone in my mouth, the second in my coat, the third in my mouth again, seeing as the first had been consumed, and I was reaching for more with both hands.

"You could do something with twenty-two fifty," the first went on.

"Maybe they'll hold out four months," I said around the sandwich.

"Four months?" That sounded unlikely to the second.

I don't know why I said what I did. I've never known why—inebriation from the taste of food maybe. I was still feeling good though, even when the cook finally noticed the way his sandwiches were disappearing into my clothing and asked in a nasty way, "What's the idea?"

"There are people waiting for these," I said, the first thing that came to mind, and absolutely true. I even pressed him a little.

"They're all jelly, too. Ain't you got any ham or something?"

"What do you need meat for? You ain't doing no work."

"You had some ham for lunch. I saw some left over." That was the first man, standing up for me, one bum for a brother. And the others joined in, everybody agreeing I should get what I want. The cook scowled but finally bent down to look behind his counter.

While he did, the financial discussion went on. The man behind me was shaking his head.

"They can't hold out four months."

"That's thirty dollars if they do," said the third.

The cook came up with some ham sandwiches, which he tossed ungraciously down on my tray. As I stepped out of line with my burden heading for the shadows, I heard the conversation concluding.

"What would you do with thirty bucks?" the second man was asking.

"Buy me an oil lease and retire," answered the first, and everybody got a good laugh out of that one.

I stowed the sandwiches about me as I walked and ditched the tray, heading for the perimeter in a beeline. Nobody said boo to me and I was soon beyond the last line of tents and back in darkness. I skirted the base of the dome for a while until the lights of the camp were out of sight behind the slope. Going back to my hands and knees, I moved in quietly toward the wire and then went flat altogether. I'd caught a glimpse of a fire through the brush, which explained why I'd gotten off the dome so easy in the first place—those men who should have been walking their beats were preferring to spend their time in each other's company, off their feet and warm. I made another wide loop around them, further around toward the far side of the dome, listened for a long while and, hearing nothing I shouldn't have, at last made my move for the wire, stuffing another sandwich in my mouth for a final bit of energy.

There was the wire—what with the full canteens and the bulging pockets I couldn't have crawled underneath, and feeling home free anyway, I began to climb the strands in plain sight. At that moment, a flashlight beam hit my face and a voice cried, "Hold it!"

I twitched. I was off balance, straddling the wire, and when I went for my gun, the dumb canteens were dangling in my way.

"Hey, now . . ." spoke the voice—he'd seen my moves. I went rigid, the sandwich hanging from my mouth, breath held. And dry-mouthed too, despite all that water—the cockiness was gone.

"Okay now—step back on this side," said the voice coming closer, and I could see a rifle barrel. I climbed down and raised my hands, all sorts of wild and surely deadly schemes running through my head. It was a true shame—I'd come so far and done so well.

"Hi, Mase," said the voice, turning the flashlight on its own face.

Oh shit, I thought—it was Marion again.

"Marion. Turn that thing off," I said.

He did so willingly. "I thought you was up there," he began. He must have realized that was a dumb thing to say, because he added, "But you're down here now, ain't you?"

So there we were, together once more and each as thrown by it as the other. We stood there for the longest while, neither of us knowing what to say next.

"How are things going?" he said at last.

"Not that great. How about with you?"

He shrugged. "Same thing. Lots of people are ready to pack it in. It's not bad work, but it's awful dull."

"Why don't you quit?"

"They won't let us. Say they'll track us and bring us back if we try to leave. I don't know—there's something rotten about the whole job, even if it is their land in the first place."

"Is that what they told you?"

"Yeah . . . Why—isn't it?"

"No."

"They didn't tell us that." He paused. "I'd almost rather be with you than down here."

I didn't respond to that, and seeing as I didn't, he didn't press it.

"Hellman's really pissed at you people. He figured

you'd fold weeks ago. He'd try and take the hill again if it weren't for the Wilcox kid who holds him back, and all he knows comes from those telegrams he gets from his daddy every day. I guess the company figures it's stuck its neck out too far."

"We guessed that."

"You were right. The whole state knows about you. There was supposed to be some government people come out the other day, but the Hellmen chased them off." He paused. "They're going to just sit here and starve you out, you know that."

"They told us."

"Yeah. Well, it's pretty fucked up."

I nodded—it was interesting, but what really concerned me was what he was going to wind up doing with that rifle. He squirmed as he stood there, apparently troubled by the same problem.

"Christ, Mase—I don't know what to do."

"Don't ask me."

"I still consider you my friend—you ain't done nothing to change that. But if they ever found out I let you through . . ." Here he sighed. "These guys are real bastards."

Give Marion your ear and he'd talk for hours. I didn't want to do anything too abrupt—it occurred to me he'd mentioned something about shooting a man dead in Canada once and while I'd laughed it off at the time, I figured he could probably do it if pressed, as anyone can. Still, the longer I waited, the poorer my chances, so trying to appear more annoyed than terrified, I started to scale the wire again.

"Yeah. Well, I'm going now, Marion. You do what you have to."

He looked lost. "Just give me a second or so."

"No, Marion. I better get back." I saw his anger surging, so I added, "I'm sorry."

He shook his rifle at me. "Damn it, you better let me think for a minute."

But I was already over the wire and, taking a deep, deep breath, nodding goodbye and heading upslope. "I ain't going to argue with you, Marion," I called back, tense all over, especially in the small of my back where I figured the bullet would lodge, if it did.

"Mase!" he shouted after me.

"No, Marion."

"This ain't fair," he bawled, growing distant. He called my name again—I closed off my ears and forced my legs on, truly wanting to run, but afraid to. I heard something chunk in the weeds beside me and jumped. A rock—he'd thrown a rock at me.

I had done it. It was difficult to believe, but with that rock, I knew I had done it, been a hero, saved us all and with a trick so slick it made me dizzy just to think of where I'd been and what I'd been doing a half-hour previously. I wanted to sing—so I sang and marched up the remainder of that slope roaring through the barricade where Cleon and Lena were waiting astonished. They'd found me gone, of course, and had figured I'd deserted, but imagine their surprise at hearing me bellow and seeing me loom from the darkness, all swollen from the sandwiches stuffed about me, unslinging four dripping canteens and starting to pull out the sandwiches and load them in a cradled arm, sandwich after sandwich, from armpits and pockets and pants legs like I was some wild-eyed prairie magician, snapping his fingers and having his coat pour forth its treasures.

Cleon was the first to come to—he whooped for joy and jumped me. I took a jelly sandwich and jammed it in his laughing mouth. We hopped howling, stumbling around the dome top, hugging my cradled arm between us like it was a newborn.

Lena only stood there watching us, uncomfortable. I pushed Cleon away and crossed to her, bowing and offering her my selection.

"You go ahead," I said, with a great lewd wink. "I ate already."

She couldn't take that—she looked away. Then she reached out, daintily picked up the first sandwich her hand touched, and took a ravenous bite.

I hurrahed again, threw my entire load into the air, and let those sandwiches rain down on the three of us like whole-wheat hailstones.

16

Well, there's only one thing to do when that mood is on you and that is celebrate. Giving it a second's thought, I decided that was no less than exactly what I wanted to do at that moment, so saying, "I'm going to have a snort," and leaving it up to them to join me or not, I headed through the dark for the iron shack where Lena kept the booze, her having saved it not for anyone's good time but in case one of us got hurt and needed something to keep the pain down. I was prepared to let her try and stop me but she didn't, so I banged inside and after tearing the place apart a bit, found the bottles hidden under a floorboard and uncorking one started in.

I'd gotten the first good swig down when the door opened and Cleon entered with a awkward grin. I offered him the other bottle, which he took readily, and saluting me with it took a healthy gulp himself. Then we commenced to laugh—what with our empty stomachs, the booze hit us like a wall caving in and we were shortly well drunk, singing "Rye Whiskey" and "Buffalo Gals" in bad harmony, sipping with one hand and munching jelly sandwiches with the other. I didn't know where Lena was, and didn't much care.

But then the door opened once more and there she stood. She took in the scene, me flat on her bed with a silly smile on my face, Cleon leaning back in a chair with his boots up on her table, which he quickly removed in an embarrassed way, and sniffed. She looked down at the two half-empty bottles with some disappointment.

"I'm celebrating," I said. "You got anything against celebrating?" I could hear my own voice and it sounded like I was talking through a bag of something.

"I'm going off shift," she said calmly. "Somebody's got to watch the rig."

She looked at Cleon but he was glancing away and giggling at something.

"Didn't you hear me?" Now Cleon turned to her, blinking. She nodded at me. "Well, he's in no shape."

Finally he got the picture. "Oh. Sure, Lena. My pleasure," he answered, took his coat, and headed for the door. Then he paused, came back, and picked up her tin hat. He stuck it on his head at a cocky angle and left grinning, delighted to be finally getting his hands on the rig, even if only by default.

Lena turned to me—I gave her another big boozy wink.

She snorted. "How long do we get to see that shit-eating grin?"

I only laughed, so she left as well, slamming the door behind her.

I laughed again, but then I stopped short. That bothered me, that slamming door. That was unkind, uncalled for. I thought about it—then I picked up my bottle and followed her outside, realizing I still had something to say to her, in fact had had it to say for some time now. She was heading for where Cleon and I slept in the burnt-out ruins of the wooden shack, seeing as her fortress had been broached and occupied, and when she heard me behind her, she quickened her pace. Still, my stride was longer and I managed to block her with my arm just as she was about to duck beneath the tarp we'd laid over the charred uprights.

She drew herself up to full defensive stance. "I was wondering when you'd get around to this."

At first I didn't get her meaning—when I did, I chuckled, it being amusing. "You didn't think I could pull it off, did you?" I said.

"I'm obliged to you," she answered, very evenly.

"C'mon—you didn't. Tell the truth, now."

"I'll pay you back." She pushed my arm aside. "Some other way."

"It was something to behold," I went on. "I walked through that camp arm in arm with Jesus Christ."

She started to enter again, but I held her back.

"I don't know why," she said. "It won't be no fun for you."

"You don't know what I'm talking about."

"Oh, c'mon . . ."

"You don't know what I want."

"A man does something fancy, and drinks, and starts feeling randy . . ."

"You don't know what I want."

"I know what men want."

"You don't know what *I* want!"

"All right, then," she shouted. "What do *you* want?"

In a very soft voice, I said, "I want you to put your arms around my neck and kiss me on the mouth and say, gee, Mase, you're a good guy after all."

She said nothing. "You ain't that drunk," she muttered finally.

"Can't cut it, huh," I said, taunting.

She blushed red and turned her back on me. We both knew what I was asking for was the hardest thing in the world she had to give, harder to give than just her body, which, after all, a long list of men had sampled. I offered her the bottle over her shoulder.

"If this will make it any easier for you . . ."

"I never drink," she said, miserable.

Now she turned back to me. "You may say I've been real nasty to you. Maybe I have, but I've got my reasons . . ."

Oh shit, I thought. After all that—words! I groaned. "I do!"

"You ain't that special."

"That ain't up to you, is it?"

Well hell, even a party alone was better than this, so I gave up whatever it was I'd had in mind and started back toward the iron shack.

"I'm trying to explain something to you," she called after me.

"You want to talk, go to your pa. He loves to talk."

I heard her coming behind me and stopped. She stepped around to the front of me. After a pause she put her arms around my neck and shut her eyes.

"What was it?"

"What I said was, gee, Mase, you're a good . . ."

She nodded. "I remember." She paused again, "Mase, you ain't such a bad guy."

And with that, she kissed me. It wasn't a lover's kiss, but then it wasn't the kiss of somebody dangling over the Grand Canyon either. It was in between—her lips were hard but she held them on mine longer than she truly had to. She couldn't look me in the face when it was over.

"Thank you," I said. "Good night."

She was bewildered. "That's it?"

"That's all."

And I walked on, all smug. Oh I had had her, I had raped her through, and she stood there dazed like any other virgin, wondering just how it had come about. I felt even better than before.

"It ain't that easy for a woman in this world," she yelled at my back.

Without turning, I answered, "It ain't that great for a

man neither, let me tell you," and with that, me and my bottle disappeared inside her shack once more, leaving her there.

The proverb goes that it's always darkest before dawn, but I would say it's the other way around, that it's always brightest just before sunset, because on that very night of my triumph, and near dawn as a matter of fact, the roof fell in. And it happened to Cleon too, though not at all his fault, since he had sobered up quickly enough in the night air and was doing just what he should have been, sitting by the cable and minding the temper screw, when the walking beam suddenly jammed stuck in mid-swing with a crash, the cable jerked rigid, and the engine, still trying to move something frozen, began to whine and howl. Cleon moved in every direction at once, bellowed for Lena and me, ran back to the winch and tried to kick it out of gear, but the strain on the drum had locked it firm and the engine was smoking and throwing showers of sparks all over him as it angrily ground itself apart.

He raced back to the cable—it was stretched taut and humming like a violin string plucked. The lumber of the derrick was creaking and popping under the strain. Then, from all the way down the hole, there was a sharp crack and the walking beam banged limp the engine, with the strain relieved, coughed and stalled.

Cleon heard a strange whooshing noise, got scared, and leapt off the platform just as the entire drilling cable, all nine-hundred-odd feet of it came shooting up the casing, whipping like something alive over his head, smashing crates, snapping at the derrick legs, searching for him for a moment before it found the derrick itself and twined itself around, wrenching the uprights under its squeeze, and then with one mighty last jerk, whipping up and through the crown block far overhead and falling in great sighing loops on the platform floor.

The ruckus had awakened both Lena and me and we stumbled over from two directions, each still groggy, her from sleep and me from my drinking.

"What did you do?" I asked him.

He rubbed his eyes and looked at the wreckage. "I got no idea."

In the silence we could hear something rising from the camp below, and after listening, it was clear it was cheering. Looking past the barricade, we could see them all coming out from their distant tents and in a sleepy way milling around in clumps to hear the good news. The Hellmen were shouting something—now a band of them ran over to a van and spread the rear doors. More shouts and a bunch of men followed. They were handing out rifles—we could tell that just by the rattle they made.

What had happened was that the rig had swallowed its tools. In the course of its progress far down the hole, the drill edge had wedged on something—the walking beam, not knowing that, still tried to pull the string upward, put all that tension on the cable, and then jammed itself. Since nothing could move, something had to snap and it was the cable, stretched like a rubber band

and doing what rubber bands do when they're stretched too far. Now this was a common enough event in the business and there were special tools to fish out the broken string, but they all called for a straight pull down from the crown block. We no longer had anything reeved through the crown block. And while that should have been simple to remedy, meaning somebody climbing the tower with a light line and threading the cable back through, at that moment a slug took an inch out of a crosstie above our heads and another gouged a derrick leg, showering us with splinters. It was clear those below knew our problem well and climbing the derrick was one task they were not going to let us accomplish.

For lack of something better to do, I walked over to the engine and, taking it out of gear, tried to start it. It spun obligingly on my first crank. I shut it down again.

Back at the platform, Cleon was staring up at the crown block. He turned as I came back.

"Any way to do it?"

He meant besides somebody going up there. I shook my head. Not as far as I knew.

17

I don't know how long we wandered in gloomy circles around that dome top, each too down to speak and too beaten to think of anything besides failure. It seemed difficult to conceive, since we were all whole and quick and still in full possession of the property, that we were finished, that the siege of Apache Dome was ended, that the party was over so to speak, but it certainly was all true, for here was the cable at our feet and there over our heads was the empty pulley, far apart, and the occasional pot shot wanging off the derrick just went to prove it all.

After a while, even pacing seemed useless, and Lena

slumped down on the platform and hid her face in her hands. I myself was aware my stomach was still queasy, so I flopped down against the stack of gas drums, just looking up at the night sky as if the answer might come from there. Only Cleon kept on the move, roaming about the dome top, picking up things and putting them down, turning things over with his toe.

I shut my eyes. Well, okay, I thought. All right. It was over.

I heard Cleon calling to Lena. He called again—still too tired to open my eyes, I just listened and heard her finally answer "what," and then shuffle over to the far side of the dome from where he was calling.

Then I heard nothing further for a time, so I got up and looked. They were both standing and pointing at the stack of curved cast-iron plates, those left from the rest we'd planted in the barricade. He was explaining something with his hands—he tried to lift the top plate off the stack but it was too heavy, so he put his shoulder behind it and it toppled off into the dust with a thud.

I couldn't figure out the point he was making, so I wandered over, in time to hear Cleon asking her, "What do you think?"

After a pause she nodded, bent down, and got her fingers under one end of the plate. Cleon got a grip on the other—together they lifted and crab-fashion scuttled it along over to the derrick, where they leaned it against an upright with a lot of puffing and mutual advice.

"What's the idea?" I asked.

Neither answered–Cleon had gone off in one direction to look for something, Lena another. He'd found it, a length of light rope, and came back, took a couple of turns around the plate widthwise, and tied a pipe hitch. Then leaning back against the plate, he started lashing himself to it.

Now I understood. It was going to be a shield.

Lena had been off hunting the same thing, but she dropped her rope, furious, when she saw Cleon had beaten her to it. "Get out of there," she shouted, ripping the loops off his body and shoving him out of the way with her hands. Glowering, she began to tie herself in, just as he had.

Cleon acted in kind once he got his balance–he pushed her aside and grabbed his rope back. Now she snatched up the other end, and they both started to pull at once in a tug of war.

"Its' my idea," he bawled.

"Don't be dumb!" She heaved hard, and he went to his knees.

"Damn you!" she cursed.

"Well, I want to!"

She heaved again, but he wouldn't let go. With that she dropped her end, took one long stride to him, wound up, and slugged him fair in the face. Cleon looked stunned, and his nose trickled blood.

"It's my well!" she yelled at him. "It's still my well!" She looked around, blowing a length of hair out of her face, challenging us both. "What's the matter with you people?"

I just shrugged. I couldn't imagine where their energy was coming from. But while she was raging, Cleon had taken the opportunity to get hold of the rope and was mulishly strapping himself once more.

She wound up and slugged him again, twice, right hand and left. You could tell by the sound they hurt—Cleon winced, but carried on stubbornly. Screaming now, she swung again from her boot tops and decked Cleon with a right hand that could have stopped a man twice his size.

He fell back on his ass, blood oozing from his mouth as well. And then something happened to his eyes—they changed their shape, from round to flat or square to rectangular, I'm not sure, but I'd seen it happen in other men, and it signified something inside Cleon had finally, after all this time and all that punishment, snapped.

Lena stiffened a little—she must have been familiar with that look as well, but defiant, she stood with both fists balled in his path as Cleon once more picked himself up and staggered toward the plate.

When he was four feet off, she cocked her arm—at three feet she swung, but that old man, showing timing I didn't know he had, blocked it with his forearm, closed, and slipping his arm under hers, drew her hard against him and locking his hands together behind her back, commenced to squeeze.

She kicked, flailed, she swore in his face and sunk her teeth into his ear but he didn't let loose. He just squeezed harder from the shoulders and the elbows, with all his might, and some stranger might have mistaken it for a father hugging his long-lost daughter, except for the fact that her curses were turning to gasps. Her fists began to lose their force and now went flat, trying desperately to push free. "Let me go," she wheezed, a true fear now in her eyes, but he only hung on like some old bulldog, gasping and red all over from the exertion. Now her arms dropped—she began to go limp, her legs buckled, and Cleon finally let her fall to the ground where she panted helplessly, trying to get up on one arm and then that arm collapsing underneath her.

Just as fast as it had come on him, Cleon's rage vanished. He leaned down by her, rubbing her back awkwardly.

"You just lost some wind, Lena. You'll be fine in a second."

I had been simply staring at all this, forgotten by both. Now he looked over at me.

"I ain't gonna have trouble with you. . . ?" He truly appeared ready to take me on as well.

I shook my head—it was all right with me.

Muttering something, Cleon returned to his business at the plate and commenced to lash himself in once more, slipping in wadding where the line looped over his shoulders.

Lena looked up at him and spoke, but no sound came out of her mouth. She took on a dazed, puzzled look, since I suppose her voice had never before betrayed her like that.

"This is important to me, Lena," Cleon said as he worked. "So I hope you'll excuse me." He took another turn over his shoulder, stuffed that with a rag, and tied a final hitch around all the ropes meeting at his chest. He tested the tension—satisfied, he stepped away from the derrick leg, taking up the weight of the plate, but I could have told him his lash-up would never work, since the plate merely sagged against the loose ropes and slid past his ass and thunked on the ground at his heels.

"That's terrible," I said—it was, being such a comic finish to such a long build-up. He blushed despite himself. I walked over, undid the knot, relooped the line till it was close to cutting his shoulders in two, then putting my foot on his chest, hauled in on the rope like rigging a packhorse. He yelped from pain.

"You feel it?"

"Yeah," he said, choking.

"Then it's right."

There was a bubbling sound which, when we turned to see, proved to be Lena again, on her hands and knees, still trying to get her voice to work. I handed him the coil of rope she'd found, tying a free end to one of his belt loops.

"When you get there, I'll splice on the cable, and you'll thread it through."

He nodded—it was simple enough. Helping him with the plate, I guided him around to the ladder and, shoving from behind, up onto the platform.

"Make him stop," Lena gasped, her voice finally coming around.

Cleon shook his head.

"He knows what he's doing," I added.

"He'll just get himself hurt."

We were both taken up by that—coming from Lena, it was like undying love from somebody else. He must have really gotten to her.

Cleon only smiled. "No, I feel good, Lena. I really do." And he did look good—in fact, he seemed more relaxed and alert than I'd ever seen him. I lifted his arms and he gripped the highest rung. He set his feet—getting under him with my shoulder, I boosted him up.

He paused there on the first rung, giving me a warm, sad look, which I suppose was gratitude. I looked away—it wasn't called for anyway, so I just slapped him on the butt for luck and stepped back to let him go at it.

He took a deep breath, let it out, set his mind, and hauled himself up a rung, wincing as the plate sagged and those ropes cut into his shoulders. Another breath and another rung, then another—the best picture I can give is that of a man climbing with the lid to his own coffin strapped on his back, if you can imagine a coffin lid of cast iron weighing maybe a hundred and twenty pounds. And it was tricky because the heavy plate still swung somewhat loose in its lashings, and as he'd throw his weight to one side in the act of climbing, the heavy thing would keep on swinging in that direction and try to pull him off the ladder altogether, so he had to climb carefully and straight, using his arms mostly and not his hips.

Lena and I stood still and silent, just watching as he rose. If she wanted to stop him, she still lacked the strength, and while I could have, I didn't want to. Bullets started to chew up the derrick again and whine through its trusses all around him, so they must have seen him in camp, or at least something moving in the darkness.

For maybe twenty feet he climbed upward in peace through that storm of bullets, unhit, and I can imagine Hellman's rage, down there in camp, seeing one man setting about to repair our damage against his twenty rifles firing in ragged order. Then there was a clang, meaning the plate had been struck—we could see Cleon drawing in his legs and arms behind it like a tortoise. More bullets found their target as the sharpshooters adjusted their aim, but the plate seemed to be serving its purpose since Cleon kept up a slow but steady progress. When I looked over at Lena, she was chewing her knuckles.

About halfway up he stopped, surely the exact wrong place to do it with the bullets flying, but he was probably well winded by then and seeking to gather his strength for the second half. He seemed to be looking down at us, and on the chance he was, Lena waved up at him hesitantly. Then he jerked, leaned back, and looked in the act of falling—he'd been hit surely, in the hand or arm, and it must have taken everything he had with the other hand and the muscles in his legs to catch himself and not topple, but somehow he did, and now he crouched up tight behind that plate while he did something, which I took as dealing with the wound. After some time, he started to climb again, but much slower, with minutes of rest in between each rung.

It was then I became aware the firing had stopped. That was strange, especially if they'd seen him struck, and I was puzzled for a moment until I happened to turn to the east and saw the first flush of dawn moving up over the horizon. A chill hit me when I figured it out—the Hellmen weren't going to waste any more rounds on a target in the dark. They'd get him clean when he was well lit by daylight, now a matter of minutes away.

In the meantime, Cleon had kept climbing—Lena and I could see him just below the hole to the water table. With one last thrust and a grunt I heard where I stood, he shoved himself through and then flopped out of sight, hid to us by the platform around the crown block, but I could imagine him easy enough, lying there with his blood thundering. The light was spreading slowly—now we could begin to make out shapes—a movement far above and a scrape of metal on wood told us he was raising the plate with his arched back and leaning it against the gin pole to make a sort of shelter for himself. Then nothing happened for a long while, but just as I began to fear that had been his final act, down the center of the derrick dropped the pull rope.

I gave him my loudest cheer. Lena was practically applauding for joy—cupping her hands, she shouted up the derrick, "How are you?"

We heard no reply, but shortly saw a white handkerchief waving over the opening, and then just after, Cleon himself stretching out over the drop and beginning to reeve the rope through. While he did his work, I did mine, splicing the rope to the cable end in a hurry—the splice was soon well secured and I trusted he would be as sure with his hands. But then the crown block began to creak and the line to the cable tightened while a new free end gradually wriggled down from the top. I'd already told Lena to crank up the engine—as the new end fell within my reach, I jumped up and snatched it, pulled it over and fastened it to the sand drum. I signaled to Lena—she put the engine in gear and we had the pleasure of seeing the cable raise up the center of the derrick like a snake awakening, pass through the crown block, and drop back down the other side and coil around the sand drum, where it would be safe enough until we could transfer it back through and onto its proper home on the bull wheel.

At this point, Cleon's work was finished and he could relax. He must have had a lovely view, all of Oklahoma below him rosy in the young sunlight, and I imagine he enjoyed it to his ability until his eyes wandered down onto the Hellman camp and answered the question of why no one was shooting at him anymore. He could see twenty men in military formation waiting patiently to fire in volley as soon as he started down, ready to blast him off the tower now that they could aim easily at a range of maybe two hundred yards, nothing special for someone who knew his weapons.

He must have seen those men—we didn't, not thinking to look, so busy were we storing the cable properly, but after some minutes it occurred to us he'd made no move.

"Maybe he's hurt more than we know," Lena said.

I decided to ask. "Can you come down?" I shouted up at him.

No answer—just the handkerchief again.

He was scared of something—that was obvious enough —probably that he didn't have the strength to carry the plate once more. But there was faster ways down, if he wanted to chance them.

"Slide down on the cable," I shouted again.

A paüse—then his winded voice replied, "It's too oily."

He was right—I felt dumb for having suggested it. Still wondering what was keeping him, I crossed to the barricade and peered down at the camp, and saw, spread below, the Hellman firing squad. I called Lena over.

"Christ," she whispered, when she saw them.

He was stuck up there, that was sure. If he didn't come down, he'd starve—Hellman would be satisfied with either. I had a vision of Cleon living the rest of his life up there among the crows, and then it occurred to me there was nothing to do but someone going up and fetching him.

And that was obviously me. Me myself.

I couldn't see going through the entire process with the iron plate again, so I told Lena to start the engine and when I said to, winch me up to the peak on the cable. She regarded me for a moment, then nodded and ran toward the engine while I pulled on some gloves and began to struggle with the greasy cable, trying to knot a piece of it for a footloop.

"What are you doing?" The voice was Cleon's, far

off, aware we were up to something. I didn't answer him.

"No, Mase–I'm coming," he called down.

Looking up, I could see the plate lifting–he was getting back into his harness again. I motioned to Lena to take slack in a hurry. The crown block creaked as the line rolled through.

"Just stay up there," I yelled back.

It might have been the grease on it or just my grip letting me down, but no matter how I swore, I couldn't get the cable to take a loop. Finally it gave, and I jammed one foot in the hold and took a grip with one hand above, shouting to Lena to haul away.

Once more, her lousy equipment let us down–the gearing could only wind in cable at a slow rate, and we both stood there twitching while it went to taut in its own sweet time.

Above us Cleon was yelling–I couldn't make out what. Glancing up, I saw the worst was happening–he was indeed back in harness and his feet were dangling over the water table, his toes searching for the ladder rungs. This was what those in camp had been waiting for. Those feet.

Their first volley ripped loudly over the engine noise, and of those twenty slugs, most of them struck home because Cleon jerked in a number of directions and, crying out, hugged the ladder, holding on with everything now. Lena screamed.

While I watched, the cable had begun to lift me up, but now I realized I was swinging five feet above the platform and traveling no higher. I yelled at Lena again, but no use—she'd left the engine and was stumbling toward the platform, head thrown back, shrieking, "Go back! Go back!" over and over.

"Haul me up," I hollered, trying to be heard over her own hollering. A second volley slammed into Cleon, shredding the rig peak—if he wasn't dead now, he was surely dying. An odd chunk of cast iron plummeted down, bouncing off the trusses as it fell—the plate itself was cracking under the force of all that lead.

"Go back—please go back," Lena sobbed, her voice sunk to a whisper now. A third volley struck him—he didn't move, but I think it wasn't the slugs so much as that damn cast iron that killed him because as his blood flowed, so did his strength, and we could see his body dropping and slumping lower on the ladder. As it dropped, the plate sagged to one side, and while before he might have had the muscle remaining to right himself, he didn't anymore and the plate kept swinging, all that metal pulling at his arms, stretching his fingers, and those shot-up fingers finally had to let go, and he fell backward, the plate first, dragging him after, off into space in a silent arc that traced forty feet and ended in a puff of dust and a pile of broken man and scrap iron at the derrick's base.

I looked. I looked and felt my eyes filling with water, and this time, for one time in my life, I didn't do what I usually did to stop them and I let them flow. I began to cry, still hanging there in midair as useless and needless as I have ever been in my life, crying and crying and saying "Oh shit. Oh, shit. Shit, shit, shit . . ." over and over again.

And I kept crying, I stayed crying, even when I let myself down and found I had no stomach for words or even for standing, and so just slumped against the sampson post, more than crying, weeping now. It was all such a shitty, shitty shame.

And as for Lena? Nothing. She sat on the platform looking at something far off, her fingers playing with each other, dry-eyed, not screaming, not talking, doing absolutely nothing at all. The man was in pieces maybe fifteen feet from her and she was doing nothing. I couldn't believe her—despite all she'd shown me, despite the fact I should have known all she was by then, I still couldn't believe her and stared at her, not even having the words to tell her why, like she was something that had come out of the hills and spoke only the language of beasts.

She was aware of me—totally composed, she stood and walked back to the engine and shut it down so as not to waste any gas. Thinking of gas led her to unscrew the cap on the gas tank and check the level with a stick. She spotted an oil leak somewhere on the block and wiped it off with a rag. That done, she wandered back to the platform, sat, took the makings out of the bib pocket of her overalls and began to roll herself a cigarette.

I'd never seen anything like it.

"Can't you even cry for him?"

"I never cry," she answered evenly, lying.

She poured some tobacco from the bag onto the paper, put the bag aside. She spread the tobacco evenly with two fingers. Then her hand began to shake.

"I didn't ask him to . . ."

The paper rattled—the tobacco scattered everywhere. And then she burst and it all came out, in a great painful moan and an explosion of tears, sobs, and a writhing body, at long last crying the cry for everything, for what she was and had ever been, getting maybe a lifetime's worth of filed and stored tears out of her body all at the same time.

She picked herself up and staggered over to where Cleon lay and flopped down beside him. "Daddy, Daddy," she moaned while she beat his bent body all over with her fists. From her voice, I couldn't tell if she was angry with him for having left her just then or the first time, twenty-five years back.

We buried that poor old man without discussing it, finding each other with shovels in our hands some point later on and going off to a spot away from the rig for the hole so we wouldn't be in his way in the future. We were stunned and sullen, although we had no right to be since his fate was no more than what we had expected all along in some far side of our minds, but then we had played that trick on ourselves everybody plays with death, even the prisoner walking to the scaffold who somehow expects to watch himself hang along with the rest of the audience. But that trick was out of the question now, since one of us was truly and finally gone. Nobody would ever see Cleon Holder again.

I call him a poor old man, but looking back that's probably too harsh, since after all, he had died in a manner of his own choosing and gotten what he wanted out of Lena by doing it, so wherever he was, he couldn't have been too upset with the bargain he'd struck. We'd lost more than he had. I threw a tin hat in the grave as we shoveled him over—it may seem like a dumb gesture, but we had lots of those hats lying around, so it didn't cost us anything.

Getting the rig back in shape was less trouble than it could have been. We sent down a spear first on the cable, a pointed tool with sawteeth that working up and down finally cut through the manila cracker at the rope socket, and drawing it out carefully, tangled itself among the rope and allowed us to fish that from the hole. As for the tool string proper, there was a device called a slips that would lower over the protruding end of the rope socket like a grapple and then close itself by triggering an internal spring, and with that firm grip, we were able to give a number of good yanks to the tools which finally tore loose and came clanking swiftly up and out of the hole as innocent as the masturbating choirboy. All this had scarred and chewed up the bore at the point where the tool string had wedged, so we tossed gravel and fine cast iron down the hole to fill it up a foot or so, then lowered and set the normal string again, boring a clean hole through that fill, and that accomplished, tying off the cable to the temper screw and putting it on the walking beam once more.

We worked smoothly, Lena and I, her doing the solving and I most of the labor, not talking much and getting things done in the simplest way. To do otherwise would have been to think about Cleon and we didn't want to do that, though not out of heartlessness. It seemed of our two choices, work was the better. By that evening we were in operation, and while I tended the cable, Lena went off to her shack to get some rest.

My notion had been to stay awake as long as I could, then shut down and sleep on the platform, but for obvious reasons I couldn't sleep that night, and so sat alone in the cold, wrapped in a blanket with only a fire in a drum at my side for company. I missed Cleon, missed the sight of him where my eyes wandered, but I also felt somewhat cleaned by his going, lighter somehow, as though matters were getting simpler and simpler all the time. That was to my taste now, the notion of less and less and less. I could see how it would all end, and knowing the end so well brought a kind of calm.

Then I heard Lena calling my name. Turning, I could see the glow of a lamp in her shack. She called once more, a bit louder.

"What?" I shouted back.

A pause, then she called my name again. Just my name.

"What do you want?" I yelled, but I knew, knew

damn well what, just from her voice. And I wasn't even surprised.

I shut down the engine, wiped the grease off my hands with a little gasoline, and started for the shack. The light went out inside—when I got to the door, I paused to knock, but figured that wasn't necessary and just stepped inside.

Opening the door sent a shaft of moonlight across the room and onto the bed, where Lena was sitting with her hair combed out. Her look was uneasy—it wasn't natural for her to be doing this, even though it was what she needed and what we both did. When I shut the door, the room was dark as coal again.

I stripped down, unhooked my overalls, pulled off my boots with a thunk. The cold bit me all over—I took a step toward where I remembered the bed had been and stubbed my toe smartly on something, swearing.

"Where are you?" I said.

"Over here."

Guiding on her voice, I found the bed. My touch told me she'd drawn back the sheets so I stretched out beside her, the bed giving a big rusty creak from the double load.

I remember full well what followed that night, every twitch and slither, remember it as well as I remember anything, and could describe it in detail did I not think it wasn't anybody's business but my own.

18

And so by next morning, we were lovers, but not so as anybody could notice, since having more or less agreed we were, there wasn't much to do about it, there being no shady groves by a river's side or goose-down beds in some honeymoon hotel within two hundred miles. Drilling that hole was both our occupation and our recreation, and though I moved into her shack at night, we'd maybe have the strength left for a nod and a touch on the shoulder before we both sank into a dazed and utter sleep. We grew kinder to each other, she having run out of things to prove to me, and me things to prod her on, and both having let go somewhat, we met in the middle at a sort of silent friendliness. With Cleon gone, we took no more trouble to guard the dome, and though Hellman could have taken us whenever he chose, it was clear he preferred to let us suffer and die in our own time, both to keep his hands clean and to give a plain example to any fools like us further down the line just what lay in store for them.

Not that Hellman was getting away untouched. The same burning summer sun beat down on all of us, and taking a few minutes to study the camp, you could notice changes. Small things—tents sagging against loose guy ropes, garbage and old newspapers blowing through the lines when the odd breeze puffed, little junk sunshades around the barbed wire where the guards dozed. I once took the time to do a head count and calculated there were maybe ten men missing over the original number. I could have been wrong, they could have been sick or fired, but the fact the Hellmen had shifted their tents over to the far side of the camp near the road and tended to cluster there during the day led me to believe at least some men had reneged on their contract, and the Hellmen had taken up their new position to block the rest from following after. And where there had been in the beginning two water wagons arriving each day to supply the camp's needs, now there was one and on some days none at all, which meant maybe the cost of running his household was getting to Hellman and he was cutting back, so if we were dying of thirst, those in camp were at least thirsty.

And then one morning, as if it was something prearranged, we woke to see another car in Deke Watson's camp by the road, and another tent, and showing its dust far off, another car on the way. By night, two more newcomers had shown up and we could hear the laughter rising from around the new, bigger campfire as all those old scouts got together to swap news, a lot more happy at their trade than the bums around their fires a half-mile off, who no longer made a sound. There must have been ten oil companies represented—it was like a crowd gathering at a finish wire, which of course was exactly the case.

Our sandwiches only stretched two weeks, the water ran out slowly, and then one afternoon when we were at 1,210 feet and into a soft lime, the gas was gone. The engine started to miss—we knew what it meant and moving slowly, since it hurt us to walk now, both inside in the belly and outside from the frayed flesh between our legs and aching joints, we went through all the cast-off empty gas drums, tipping them for the odd drops collected at the bottoms, wiping them out with a rag and wringing it into a pot, gathering maybe a cup's worth, which we poured carefully into the gas tank. The engine picked up, its beat smoothed out, and it ran evenly for another ten minutes or so, maybe five hundred more strokes of the walking beam and an equal number of bites of the bit, and then the engine gave three sharp coughs and quit for good.

I'd prepared for this moment a week earlier, fashioning a long crank with two handles out of round stock that fit the dog of the engine's starter pulley. Unbolting the engine's head to break all that compression, we found we could, by both heaving together, spin the engine. We unhooked the drilling cable from the walking beam and used it as a jerkline, simply lifting the cable and string up the hole by cranking the engine, which in turn revolved a cable winch with a toothed wheel and a check pawl, a hinged thing like a finger that would catch on the wheel's teeth as each passed. We'd measure our progress by the clicks of the pawl, winding up that cable tooth by tooth and click by click, with each click calling for our total joined srength. Twenty clicks were five feet of lift to the tool string—then we'd knock the pawl free with a hammer, the cable would unreel and the string down the hole would hit, and bite of its own weight. What the engine had done thirty times a minute, we could do twice an hour if we felt good. At that rate we'd reach 2,000 feet in the same year—it was truly the most thankless labor I've ever performed.

But as I've said, what was eating at us was eating at those in camp. That same night, as I sat dozing on the rig platform and Lena slept beside me, I heard a commotion from far off and waking her, we both staggered over to the rim to look. There was more activity in camp than there'd been in weeks—clumps of men here and there, men running and chattering back and forth, going in and out of their tents. After a while, all the movement took on meaning—the bums had decided to leave, for soon those separate groups gathered together in a mob and started out for the road with shouts of "c'mon, c'mon," only to be halted by a line of others, which we couldn't see well but could easily guess were the Hellmen. We expected gunfire—instead, there was a parley between the two crowds while both shouted angry things at each other, and piecing together what came to us, it was clear we were witnessing a mutiny. Maybe those fifty men were tired of what they were doing—maybe they were only tired of watching the cable fall every fifteen minutes or so and knowing what we were going through to cause that.

Were it up to Hellman, he surely would have gunned them down where they stood, but young Wilcox still held the reins, however weakly, and where Pan-Okie was not opposed to the odd murder, it probably couldn't go so far as a massacre, which was the only alternative to letting the bums go. After more parley, the Hellmen line grudgingly split in two and the bums, slowly at first, being properly worried, passed through them. The line of Hellmen closed behind and prodded them along like drivers at a rabbit hunt, before anxious to hold them but now anxious to see them on their way. And I could guess Hellman's reasoning—faced with this situation, the best he could ask for was to get the bums out fast, hopefully before we found out about it, and somehow fake their absence when daylight came so we wouldn't take any heart from their leaving. It wasn't bad thinking—once they saw they weren't going to be harmed, the bums quickened their pace, passing through the scouts' camp like a herd around a haystack.

But at some point, with darkness and freedom just at hand, some of them must have likewise gotten Hellman's drift, and no longer wanting to do anything to aid him, stopped and shouted something up at the dome. At first we didn't realize it was meant for us until a few of the bums got together and shouted in unison, loud, and since the rig wasn't working and it was otherwise silent on the prairie, clear:

"*We're leaving.*"

Now more voices joined in, first at random so all that came to us was a babble, and then sorting themselves out under one leader so their shouts broke at the same time, "*Hey—we're leaving. We're leaving,*" over and over, until a blast of rifle fire from the Hellmen line dispersed them and sent them scattering. Aside from a few more calls in the darkness from one man shouting for his buddy and some schoolboy laughter, nothing more was heard, and all was quiet once more.

Morning revealed seven Hellmen left and two or three bums who had stayed on for various sucking-up reasons. Among them I couldn't spot Marion—in fact, it had come to me the night before that his voice had been the first to call out to us and that he even might have been the conductor that led them all, but I never found out for sure, having never seen him again, and I trust he got away safely.

You could say Lena and I were angry at Hellman and his crew for the ordeal we were suffering, but it's not as if we sat around cursing his name and gnashing our teeth. We suffered, yes, but we were not victims—we had put ourselves on top of Apache Dome, not him. That was the only thing that made sense as it came to an end—that we wanted to be there, that after having beaten us and robbed us and cut us off to die, he hadn't been able to get to our bottom line, to us ourselves. I suppose I might have mulled over some plan to go down the hill again one night and kill Hellman in his sleep, but that would have been a pissy thing to do and would have gained us no relief anyway. Besides, I was not the same man I'd been weeks earlier when I'd gotten the food—I now knew I had a limited store of energy left and I could dole it here or dole it there and it seemed more sensible to save it for working that impossible rig and striking that invisible pool than something as unprofitable as simple assassination.

I was nowhere near the same man—in fact, that morning as we sweated and cranked that rigging, it occurred to me I wasn't quite sure who I was anymore. Where the night before my aching stomach had felt like I'd swallowed a bag of spikes, now it felt light and fluffy, almost as if it no longer existed. The same with my cracked tongue—it was there, in that I could feel it, but it no longer took up space, and its blisters seemed healed and smooth. I meant to ask Lena about it but it somehow slipped my mind, and we worked in silence, with me marveling at my new condition which, if it were true, meant I could work that rig for weeks more, since it seemed no longer the massive structure it had always been but now something out of spun sugar, wavering and swaying when the wind hit it, and the engine no longer a burning block of steel but some bright toy, some music box, lacking a monkey. How good I felt, it came to me, and looking up at the derrick top, I seemed to see smiles on the faces of those carrion crows, as though they agreed with me.

True, I was aware that since daybreak we two had managed together to crank that cable maybe four teeth high, with an hour of sprawling rest between each one, but that didn't matter, since I was no longer in any hurry. We'd crank it someday if not today. It was all fine.

So when the next time we gripped that crank, planted our feet, shoved with everything and all that happened was Lena's hands slipping and her dropping in the dust glass-eyed in surrender, I didn't mind because I could do it all myself.

"I'm sorry," she whispered.

"That's all right," I smiled. "Your stomach?"

"All over."

I smiled again to show her it was okay, set myself, and by jamming my feet against the base of the engine mount for purchase, managed to raise the pawl another click. Then I plopped down alongside her.

My beaming face must have cheered her because she smiled back.

"You can have that twenty-five percent now."

I had to think for a moment before I remembered what she was talking about. "Hell," I said. "I'm doing half the work. I want fifty." But that wasn't right. "Hell, I'm doing all the work."

"Take a hundred percent, then."

I shook my head. "I want a hundred and twenty-five."

"Take a hundred and fifty, if it would make you feel good." She giggled.

"Two hundred. That's what I want. I could hold up my head with two hundred percent of this oil well."

Now we both giggled. Two hundred percent–that was awfully funny. It was all awfully funny.

Her laughter made her stomach knot. "Oh, I don't feel well at all," she moaned. She moved closer to me, stretching out and putting her head in my lap. Her hair felt good to the touch, but then everything felt good to me.

"I hated you for the longest time," she said.

"You liked me from the start. When you saw me with my shirt off that first day."

"You don't look bad with your shirt off."

She paused and scratched at some peeling skin. "I bet you could still get away."

"I might."

"Do it then–if you want." She wasn't giggling now –she was serious.

I thought it over, but I couldn't come to any decision. Things kept slipping away.

"You decide," I said.

"It ain't up to me."

"I'm telling you it is."

"It ain't my choice."

"It is if I give it to you."

A little bit of the old steel came back to her eyes. "You can't do that."

"Sure I can," I said gaily. "I can do anything I want."

At that point, I truly felt I could. Still, I was concerned what her answer would be.

"If it makes no difference, then you should stay," she said, finally.

"Okay." I thought about it. "Okay."

With that I got up and addressed myself to the crank once more.

"You want to know what my first name is?"

"What?"

I winked at her. "Noble."

She giggled—I roared. I muscled that cable up another click, went around to the winch, and sledged the pawl out, letting it drop and smiling at the soft faraway chunk that came floating up out of the bore.

It must have been sometime that evening that I collapsed. I don't recall it precisely, but I do remember working the crank, listening for the scrape of rust on rust that meant the pawl was slowly raising, matching my entire weight against the drag of the winch gears, it pushing me as I pushed it, and then me gradually losing, being steadily shoved backward, and then spilling to the ground. I seem to remember just laying there, as still as Lena where she lay half-conscious by the engine, as still as the rig, as still as everything else atop that dome.

19

As best as I can determine, Hellman's mutt, Bull, and Deke Watson of Tri-State were the first two the following morning to sense something was about to happen, Bull because of his dog's hearing that picked up the first rumblings in the earth far beneath the dome, and Deke because of his scout's hearing that had became doglike over the years. Bull wasn't sure and so merely growled or whined or cocked his head, anyway nothing enough to wake his master, because Deke was first up, yanking on his trousers with one hand and shaking his partner C. R. awake with the other, then tiptoing out into first light, not waking a soul in the scout camp, even going to the trouble of putting C. R. behind the wheel of their car and shoving it a hundred yards down the road before he started it, so the engine wouldn't rouse anybody.

While they were doing that, Bull was finally making up his mind and waking his master. Hellman only had to put his ear to the ground to know what was going on—he blew his whistle loud enough to wake every man and animal within a hundred miles, everybody minus Lena and I who were still dead to the world.

The camp awoke with gummy eyes, but one man's confusion roused the other, and with Hellman, his duster over his underwear, bawling orders and his men fishing for boots and weapons and hats pell-mell, they began to sort themselves out. That shifting, groaning sound coming from below their feet was unmistakable now, and if they needed more proof, they could hear the sudden grind of Watson's car as he floored it, speeding for the dome road.

On the dome, the ground was trembling and banging—Lena woke, still so logy she couldn't connect the noise with the rig and assumed it was something the Hellmen were up to, so she carried herself over to the rim and looked down. There was Watson and Miller urging that beat-up car down the road toward us as fast as it could manage, the other scouts in their cars following far behind, some dressed, some bare-assed, some gathering speed and some cursing cold engines. In the Hellman camp, Hellman himself was at the center of things, his arms flapping wildly as he sent men here and there.

At this point, she saw young Wilcox stagger out of his tent in a dressing gown and run to Hellman. The two started arguing, but their relationship must have broken down at this point because rather than reason with Wilcox, Hellman shoved him aside and stood up on the running board of his car, shouting something Lena couldn't make out and taking a bill out of his wallet and waving it around. When he was done, his gathered men let out a whoop, some started sprinting flat-out for the slope, others piled into Hellman's car, along with Bull barking, and that laden vehicle, Hellman himself driving, bucked across the hardpan toward the same gate in the wire Watson and the scouts were making for. It looked to her like they were finally going to rush us—Hellman's speech had been to that effect and that waved bill a bounty to the first man that captured the well.

The camp emptied directly as each man raced for the dome in his own chosen way, leaving Wilcox standing there, dumfounded, until he ducked back into his tent and came out with a briefcase, and still in his dressing gown started hotfooting it after the rest, rummaging through that briefcase as he ran and casting away paper after paper until he found the one he wanted, keeping that and throwing the briefcase away as well.

Only now did Lena, still half asleep, put together the rush for the dome and that booming and rumbling all around her, and realize that her well was, in fact, coming in, and Hellman was out to seize the property before it did.

The old Lena would have grabbed her weapons and made a stand, but the present Lena could only watch in a dull way. The noise scared her—then there was a ripping explosion and a whoosh from the rig that knocked her flat. Peeking out from beneath her arms, she had the singular experience of seeing the entire string of casing we had laid so carefully, four hundred feet all nicely lowered and cemented in plate, rising slowly out of the hole like an elevator.

This served to wake me—I have been awakened rudely in my life but never more so, since I can't imagine anything less ordinary and more dreamlike than the sight through bleary eyes of an endless column of iron pipe rising on a geyser of natural gas, with a terrible screech and the sound of metal tearing, rising unstoppable at its own steady pace, reaching the height of the derrick and blocked there by the water table, beginning to buckle, the pipe joints banging as they cracked free, and the twenty-foot lengths plummeting down, only to be replaced by more pipe, and more, and now the casing beginning to fold and gather in on itself accordionlike, so that the derrick, now full up with tearing pipe, could no longer confine it, and as it always will, wood giving in to metal, with popping crossties and splintering legs, began to break apart as that mass of casing sought room to expand. With its support weakening, the entire derrick tottered more and more and then slowly and reluctantly collapsed to the ground with a massive crash that shivered the earth and raised me bodily off it for an instant. That obstacle removed, the casing continued to climb out of the steaming wreckage and I could swear it went past our four hundred feet and started on some other lengths that some other hand had set, just for the purpose of smearing our faces into the catastrophe that much more.

We may have been overcome by this, but nobody else was—at the wire, Hellman was winning the car race with Watson, though those scouts and their fellows were only yards behind him, and those in camp who had trusted to their feet rather than machinery were halfway up the slope, winded but coming on us fast.

Lena and I were staggering to each other, holding each other up like people do after a tornado takes their roof away. The casing was completely expelled and it lay in a jumbled pile over the wreckage of the rig platform. It had been quiet for a moment but now the rumbling returned, louder than ever, and building again. We held our breaths—from among the pile of casing came a little spout of mud, welling up and then falling back. Then there were a few coughs, and some rocks shot up into the air. And then, with the loudest, most gut-turning belch I'd ever heard, there was a boom and a great gout of mud and water burst over the wreckage. It spread over the dome top and suddenly stopped, like a faucet had been turned.

More silence—and a new sound more awful than any preceding—the whine of strained rock, of the entire dome tearing itself apart deep inside. The ground swayed like an earthquake was on us, but suddenly with a clap like a thunderbolt, the well exploded again and this time a yellow geyser burst flowering into the sky and arched over our heads, climbing, climbing, up to a hundred feet, then cascading over and pelting the dirt around us, yellow at first, then turning darker to brown, and as it covered us, matting our hair, making our skin glisten, we could tell it was oil, first-quality crude oil and nothing else at all.

Everyone froze, the men on the slope ten feet short of the barricade, Hellman halfway up the road—everyone just watched this thundering, roaring stream that towered over their heads like a giant tree, a weeping willow whose branches bent to the ground and left great pools of oil wherever they touched. Some of those present had seen wells blow in before, but not this one, not ours, and they gathered here and there in awestruck knots.

Of all of them, only Watson kept to business—taking the advantage of Hellman's halt, he leaned on the horn, tromped the throttle at the same time, and squeezed past on the narrow dome road, denting and shoving Hellman's car almost over the side and making a hash of his own, but not so much the motor still didn't pull them toward us, and all the other scouts followed close behind.

We were dazed and dopey—it was as if we'd wandered into somebody else's event and were waiting to be told what it was all about. Not speaking, only blinking, we saw Watson bucket toward us and skid to a stop, leap out and run through the oil puddles and the pelting oil rain with a piece of paper in his hand. It was the first time we'd seen him up close—he was a seedy old bastard with a crafty look.

"Here you go, lady. Dollar a barrel."

He shoved a contract in her face with one hand and a pen with the other.

"One twenty-five for the first ten thousand!"

Another scout had joined him. A third wedging in between the two had the presence of mind to bring a canteen along, which Lena snatched and half-emptied before passing it to me. Her voice couldn't have worked without that water to lubricate it, but now with a voice finally, she still didn't know what to say. After all this, after the years she'd put in and the months we'd gone through, in her moment of glory, she didn't know what to say and she looked from face to face as if waiting for a suggestion.

It was wonderful, it was beautiful—the gusher arced overhead like a cataract undiminished. I beamed like an idiot and when I saw Hellman standing alone, arms folded, regarding the well and muttering to himself, I couldn't resist staggering over to gloat at him a little. He saw me coming and before I could say what I'd come for, he shoved me smartly down. I had no strength to resist, so I settled for grinning up at him while sprawled at his feet.

At this point, Wilcox came puffing up to the circle of scouts, his silk dressing gown now oil-soaked and fit only for packing bearings, a contract of his own in his hand.

"Did she sign yet?"

"She's holding out." The scout who said that gave Lena a firm look. "Quick—say something, lady."

"Go ahead—what do you want?" added Deke.

"Ask anything. Rape us, lady—now's your chance," said a third.

I swear I could hear Lena's mind turning above the rush of the oil. Taking a deep breath, she answered, very slowly, "Two fifty a barrel against the first fifty thousand."

The scouts winced—everybody hesitated. Except Deke—he shoved the contract and pen back at her.

"Fill the numbers in yourself." And he presented her with his back for a writing desk.

Lena sighed, long and loud. I got up on one arm and watched her with pride. I was proud of her—she'd done it, we'd done it. You couldn't tell, what from the pain remaining and the noise and the oil that half blinded us, but she and I had won.

And so busy was I concentrating on her, my Lena, and so busy was she concentrating on that contract, that we were among the last of all those on that dome top to notice the driving rain of oil had gradually lessened—in fact, it wasn't until she had signed the bottom line of the contract with a flourish and looked up that she became aware the flow from the well had stopped altogether.

Of all of us, Hellman was the first to react. "Put it

on pump," he bawled, and in a flash that crowd of cutthroat competitors turned into a drilling team as they rolled up their sleeves and pitched in in one frantic hurry. While Hellman supervised, some hauled the crated pump out of the iron shack where it had sat unheeded all those months, some kicked the broken casing away from the platform, while others bolted a flange to a length of sound casing and manhandled it down the hole. Others siphoned gas out of car tanks and got the engine rolling, rerigging the belts and drives—by now the pump was being bolted to the flange prepared for it and its pulley being linked to the bull wheel. I staggered this way and that, trying to lend a hand, but I was paid no mind, since this was obviously a situation for professionals and not half-assed amateurs like my partner and myself.

The pump was clutched in—it ground in protest as it sucked only air. The crowd gathered around the pump outlet, all waiting. I helped Lena over to the crowd's edge—so packed was the circle that we had to stand on tiptoe to see what was happening.

Some gurgling noises came from the outlet. A gout of oil spurted out—then just dry sucking for a while. Being so occupied, none of us had noticed Watson tapping C. R. on the shoulder, guiding him out of the circle, taking a roll of instruments from their car, and heading off on their own.

A couple more gulps of oil blew free. A trickle. Then the pump was dry again, for good. Those in the circle who'd been waiting tensely now straightened up and relaxed. All were grinning—some laughed at each other and some turned around to Lena and me to laugh at us.

Lena was thunderstruck. She walked heavily to Hellman, the contract limp in her hand, her face one total question mark.

"What happened?"

"You missed the pool," answered one of the scouts.

Hellman smiled dryly. "It's your well, Miss Doyle."

Behind us, there was the sound of a car engine starting—we turned to see C. R. and Watson roaring off at full speed down the road. Then a shout from downslope came from one of the men.

Hellman put it all together.

"The old bastard took a core!"

With that, everybody came alive again—Wilcox and the scouts racing for the far slope, Hellman back to his car to fetch a map roll before he ran after. Lena and I stumbled far behind.

Halfway down the dome side, two of the Hellmen were standing around an outcrop and pointing as the others arrived. The outcrop had one sharp-cut vertical side showing all its strata, a cut that had been made with a shovel.

"It's the syncline."

"What's the dip?" cried Wilcox.

The scout eyeballed it. "Ten degrees or so."

At this point, Hellman arrived with the map and they all clutched at it, roaming it with anxious fingers.

"Back up five miles or so."

Wilcox tapped the map with his finger. "That's Osage land."

"Unleased," answered Hellman, and snatching his map, raced up the slope again with all the others following. All except Wilcox.

"You can't drill on Indian land!" he shouted. Once more he realized he was alone, at which point he got the sense to scurry after.

Blinking, I watched the first of the scouts climb over the rim and run past me toward their cars. Lena sat down in the slick dirt where she stood. I tried to think of something to say, but I couldn't. Looking around, I saw Hellman coming over the rim, about to pass me.

I found myself with a two-by-four in my hand, probably a hunk of wreckage off the rig, and taking a few paces to my side, put myself in his path, with the board poised to swing. The sight of me there stopped him—in one quick motion, his hand went for his duster pocket, but I swung and smashed it and sent flying the Derringer it had come up with.

Behind us, engines roared as five or six cars spun around in mad circles, each trying to gain the road down first. A horn was honking—it was Bliss calling to Hellman, and Wilcox was adding his voice. Hellman looked at the car, then at me who was keeping him from it.

He took a step—I swung, but not much of one, and he grabbed the board easily, took hold, pushed with his arms, and there I was, flat on my back once more. He stood over me, considering—he would have dearly loved to tromp my body into the mud, but that horn kept honking.

"Don't be ridiculous," he said at last, and planting his foot in my gut stepped off on me, squishing me flat, and hurried over to the waiting car.

Lena ran over screaming and helped me up, but I indicated I was whole enough. On every side of us the cars raced, jamming together at the bottleneck of the dome road until somebody got frustrated enough to spin out of line and dive over the rim itself, bucking and bouncing down the rutted slope with baggage and passengers flying. Others followed their lead and in an instant they were all gone. Staggering to the rim, we could see them, each one making his best time, smashing through barbed wire, hurtling ditches, flattening tents, and bowling over supplies, each raising his own rooster-tail of dust as they hit the flatland and sped off toward the northwest.

A wind picked up as we helped each other gingerly down the slope, and we had to fight our way into the abandoned camp against a flurry of blown garbage, odd clothes flapping, ashes from campfires. Two of the Hellmen had remained to pack up the gear, but they paid us no heed as we waded about through the refuse, filling up on water and food as we found it, trying to make up to our bodies for weeks of abuse.

Once fed we sat, neither knowing what to do next, although I had had more experience at handling catastrophe than she had. Finding an odd shirt, I tied the arms together to make a pouch and set out to scavenge for myself what I thought might be useful in my future—boots, a hat, some small change. I rummaged through the chow wagon and came up with, of all things, an apple. It seemed like a year since I had seen fruit but then, when I thought about it, it seemed just as long for her, so I brought it over to Lena. She devoured it, nodding her thanks.

"What are you going to do now?" she asked.

"Go to Mexico." It was like a reflex, saying that—I had no idea, actually.

She nodded.

"Are you interested?"

"That's not a bad idea," she said, mouth full. "I've heard of a place called Veracruz, and they're digging wells with picks and shovels down there."

I shook my head. "I've had enough of the oil business."

She stopped in the middle of a bite.

I shook my head again—I was serious. Her face fell somewhat.

"How about you?"

She shrugged.

"Start all over?"

"I guess so."

I nodded. My eyes drifted about—I spotted the hat of a small man I thought might fit her, so I fetched it for her. She tried it on and it worked well enough.

"Thank you."

"You're welcome."

I wanted her to say something more than that, but I wasn't going to beg. She wasn't going to say it, by her look. So there we were. She wasn't and I wasn't.

I slung the pouch over my shoulder. "Good luck, Lena," I said, and started for the country road.

I'd gone maybe fifty yards, when I heard her call my name. She was just sitting there.

ABOUT THE AUTHOR

Marc Norman currently lives in Los Angeles with his wife and children, where he writes books and movies.